Clan of the Cave Bear: The Complete Series

Clan of the Cave Bear

Ash Gray

Published by Ash Gray, 2024.

CLAN OF THE CAVE BEAR: THE COMPLETE SERIES

First edition. February 25, 2024.

ISBN: 979-8224839735

Written by Ash Gray.

Table of Contents

Taken by the Chieftess 1

Passed Around 14

Keeping Warm 28

Her Pretty Pet 41

Dominated 54

Seduced 68

Caught 78

Taken by the Chieftess

Tara knelt in the cool darkness of the cave as outside, birds sang and insects chirruped. The forest was alive in the bright Spring, but Tara was a woman now. She had full breasts jutting behind her fur hides. She had hips. She had bled. Which meant she could no longer run and play with the other young and unclaimed women. Now she must humble herself and be claimed by a suitable warrior.

There were two classes among the tribes. There were the warrior women – giant and musclebound women, who hunted, fought for territory, and protected the clans from wildlife and rival clans. These women produced offspring with their wives by fingering them – or so Tara had been told.

And then, there were the cave wives. These women were small, feminine, birthed the children, sewed the hides, and cooked the meals. Tara, as she understood it, had grown to be a cave wife. She hadn't the natural strength or size of a warrior. Oh, no. she had wide hips and big breasts, which were perfect for bearing young. Her mother was so proud, for she had feared that Tara would grow to be a warrior and thus, put herself quite often in direct danger.

Tara wasn't sure it mattered. She only hoped she would attract a suitable wife. To be taken by a worthless and lazy warrior was the worst thing that could happen to a woman. Such a warrior was a laughing stock to the rest of the tribe and were typically driven out if they could not contribute to the clan in some meaningful way. Unfortunately, there was no such thing as "divorce" among the clans, and so a cave wife was typically cast out with her disgrace of a warrior wife – unless, of course, someone else were willing to claim her.

A cave wife could not survive without a warrior wife. It was the way of things. And so, Tara sat on the cave floor, perched on her knees, and listened with quiet anxiety to the wisdom her mother imparted her as the older woman paced back and forth before in the cool darkness.

The cave had been their home for one year, for the clans were always roaming as they followed the mammoth herds. Inside, a fire pit had been dug in the center of the floor, and around it were skins and animals hides. Cooking implements carved of wood hung from the low cave ceiling, and near the barren fire pit stood the rock slab that Tara's mother often prepared meat upon. It was still stained with blood from that morning's roast mammoth.

Tara was a small young woman with messy blonde hair shorn short, a narrow waist, round hips, and great breasts. She was swathed, like all the women of the clan, in skimpy animal hides. She knelt in the half-light of the cave as sunlight reached its fingers in, and her mother, Suga, walked a stern circle around her as she appraised her.

Tara's three sisters knelt nearby, all of them younger than she. There was Firga, Marmar, and the youngest, Varg, who giggled behind her hands each time Suga fussily adjusted Tara's fur hides to make her cleavage more apparent.

Tara sighed as her mother leaned down to tug on her top yet another time. "Mother!" she complained. "I might as well go with no top at all!"

Suga straightened up with a snort. "What do you think the other girls will be doing?"

Tara blushed deeply at the very thought. That morning, all the young and eligible women in the clan would walk the mountain trail, allowing the single and eligible warrior women to get a good look at their bodies for the first time since their flowering. Potential cave wives would make themselves as appealing as possible so as to attract the best warrior wife. Many would adorn themselves with flowers and bear teeth. Tara already had a white flower pushed behind her ear, and around her throat was a choker of bear teeth that her father – the warrior woman Nutfar – had given to her the winter before her passing.

If a warrior wife saw a woman she wanted, she would simply march down from her cave, snatch said woman, and carry her off to be deflowered. Tara was terrified no one would want her at all. Being claimed by a bad warrior was terrible, but not being claimed at all – no woman had ever recovered from such a fate.

"In fact, it's tradition to bare your tits," Suga complained. She tugged Tara's top again, harder this time, as if to rip it. "Come now, take this off –!"

"Mother!" Tara gasped and wiggled from reach, eyes wide in shock.

"Just show one tit!" Suga begged, still reaching, her long gray hair swinging forward. "You have such nice tits, and if one of those warriors out there saw, why she'd snatch you up in a heartbeat—"

"Mother!" Tara wailed, and slapping her mother's hands off, she sprang to her feet and backed away.

Kneeling opposite Tara around the fire pit, Tara's three sisters stared with their mouths open, and even little Varg stopped giggling. The silence drew on, and Tara thought a look of shame crossed her mother's face.

Tara stared at her mother in amazement. She had never seen calm, dignified Suga behave so desperately before. Suga had practically ripped her out of her top!

Suga irritably folded her arms, and her long animal hides hung from them like wings. "Stubborn girl!" she scolded. "Your father, the gods bless her, has been dead since winter last. We've no one to provide for us. I'm barely holding us together!" Her expression softened and she stepped close, placing her soft hands on Tara's shoulders. "If you make a good match, your wife will provide for all of us through the coming winter. Our survival depends on you!"

Tara looked into her mother's eyes and felt a sting of guilt to see the fear and sadness there. Then she looked past her mother at her sisters, who were all watching her unhappily. Little Varg cast her eyes down and played with her fingers. Marmar sadly rubbed her arm. Firga met Tara's eyes and nodded seriously.

Firga was the dutiful grim one. She was also quite large and would probably flower into a warrior woman one day. Tara wouldn't have been surprised.

Firga, though she was younger, had always been a source of strength and encouragement for Tara. She looked at Tara from behind strings of messy hair, and when they met eyes, Tara felt her strength returning.

Tara nodded in silent thanks to Firga, then with a lift of her chin, she pulled her top off with a toss of her yellow hair, allowing her big breasts to tremble free, standing high and plump in the cool cavern air.

Suga beamed with pride as she said, "That's my girl. Catch a big one."

• • • •

OUTSIDE, WOMEN WERE already sauntering back and forth up the mountain trail, making their way past the caves where the warrior wives lived. Tara could see the big women loitering in the dark mouths of their caves. All of them were large, muscle-bound, draped in animal hides that did nothing to cover their bugling arms and strong thighs. They had wild long hair and fierce eyes, strong bodies and grim dispositions.

Tara recognized some of the warriors as already mated. It was common for some to have six, seven wives. The more wives a warrior woman had, the better a provider she typically was. But to be First Cave Wife, that was ideal. The First Cave Wife was a position of authority. She ran the family and only the warrior wife had authority over her. It was the sort of life Tara wanted, anyway, for she was the eldest of her mother's daughters and was used to having authority. She dreaded being claimed by someone who already had several wives and daughters.

Young women were already being snatched and taken, and Tara gasped at the brutality of it. But the women, contrary to being frightened, only giggled and squealed as they were snatched and tossed over the shoulders of the giant women. One dark-haired beauty was snatched up like a little doll and thrown over a big warrior woman's shoulder – so hard, her breasts were jiggling everywhere as she blushed and was carried into the darkness of a nearby cave.

After a pause, screaming always came from the caves, but it didn't sound like terrified screaming. Instead, it sounded as if the screaming women were enjoying what was happening! They gasped, begged for more, called out the names of the very gods! Tara blushed brightly as she kept walking and wondered what exactly was happening in those caves. What was about to happen to her?

Tara was walking uncertainly down the sunlit trail when a warrior suddenly came stomping down from her cave, so tall that she blocked out the sun and cast a cold shadow over Tara. Tara staggered to a startled stop and gasped: it was Scraggy, a warrior woman who was lazy, disgusting, and only had one miserable wife. She had such a poor reputation that it wouldn't be long before she was run from the clan – and she had chosen to take Tara!

Tara held back tears. Why in the name of the gods? And how could she get out of it? Scraggy was bigger and stronger, and Tara could not have refused her. Tara's heart sank when Scraggy's big hand clapped hard and hot around her wrist. The big woman leered down at her, several teeth missing, one eye smaller than the other, black hair crawling with lice. Tara cringed in horror.

"Nice big titties," Scraggy said, a bit of drool slipping down her chin. "Will be good for my children, good for me to suck as I fuck you bloody—"

"Scraggy!" boomed a voice. "She's mine! Let her go!"

Heart pounding, Tara looked around and went still in shock: Chieftess Ohana was marching toward Tara and Scraggy, a scowl on her face. Like all the warriors, she was a large woman, covered in muscles, and her white hair blew back on the breeze as she came, giving her an almost heroic appearance as the sun glowed misty behind her.

"I saw her first!" Scraggy snarled and yanked Tara close by the arm.

Tara screamed softly and staggered forward. Then Scraggy's big arm closed around her narrow waist, and in sudden anger, she twisted and gasped to get free. Her struggle only made her big breasts jiggle wildly, and when she looked up, Scraggy was looking down at her, eyes glazed with lust. To her pleasure, so was Chieftess Ohana, who had drawn near and was now standing over them.

Tara looked up at the chieftess, her heart pounding in her throat, and she swallowed hard when their eyes connected. Ohana's eyes softened with affection when they looked at her, and Tara's heart fluttered beneath the big woman's longing gaze. But as if she had caught herself, Chieftess Ohana turned her slanted eyes back to Scraggy and she scowled.

"I said," Ohana reached back and pulled her spear, "let her go."

Scraggy stared with grim determination into Ohana's face. Sneering with hatred, she gently released Tara and nudged her aside, reaching back for her own spear. But she didn't even have time to pull it: Ohana rammed her spear blade through Scraggy's neck. Onlookers screamed and shouted as blood spurted hot over Ohana's expressionless face. Then Ohana ripped the blade free and watched with satisfaction as Scraggy collapsed backward in a pool of blood.

Ohana then shouldered her spear, and when she looked down at Tara, her fierce eyes were once again soft. Tara gazed up at the big woman, completely paralyzed by lust and awe. She could see the shape of Ohana's breasts through her fur hides and wondered what they looked like, what it felt like to be in the big woman's arms. She blushed in shame at her own thoughts, and Ohana, seeing this, smiled the smallest smile. Then without a word, she lifted Tara easily by the waist and slung her gently over her shoulder. Then she turned and marched off – carrying Tara back to the cave that she shared with her daughters and wives.

• • • •

TARA DIDN'T UNDERSTAND why she had been chosen by Ohana. The chieftess already had several wives and children, some of her wives were pregnant, and with the winter coming, she certainly didn't need another mouth to feed. But for some reason or other, Ohana had chosen Tara – had killed a clan member in cold blood just to take her! – and Tara was too shocked and confused to even ask why.

When they reached the cave of the chieftess, the cave wives were chatting around a fire while their white-haired daughters ran amok, giggling and playing. Seeing that Ohana had returned with a woman over her shoulder, there was a stampede as everyone ran to her at the cave entrance. The wives kissed Ohana and doted on her, wiped her face clean of blood and asked her eager questions about Tara, while the daughters ran around behind their female father to stare up into Tara's face.

"She has huuuuge tits!" cried a tiny girl in amazement and spread her little arms with a big grin, to which Tara blushed hard.

"Do you have milk in your tits?" squeaked another girl, drawing near. She stared up at Tara with big, curious blue eyes. "My mommy has milk, and sometimes I still drink it while she's sleeping—"

"All right, that's enough," laughed Ohana. "Everyone out. Until sundown – out to the flower fields!"

Ohana's family, still laughing and chatting, left the cave without complaint, leaving the big barbarian woman alone with Tara still draped over her shoulder. Ohana then stepped close to the crackling fire and knelt down on one knee, gently laying Tara on the spread furs beside it.

Lying on her back in the nest of her yellow hair, Tara looked down past her big breasts at Ohana, who was kneeling over her and gazing down at her, eyes hard with lust. Tara felt something in her thump, felt her clitoris throb with desire. But she was nervous and afraid. What was about to happen?

Ohana leaned over Tara and took both of her big breasts in each hand, squeezing and massaging them, until the pink nipples were jutting in her large fists. Her eyes narrowed as Tara blushed, then she leaned down and sucked deeply, hungrily, on one of Tara's hard nipples.

Tara gasped and the sudden flush of pleasure made her blush, made her sex throb and squirm. She hesitated and reached out, cradling Ohana's white head to her breasts, so that the soft cleavage rose in a mound against the warrior's face. This pleased Ohana, who suckled more deeply, mouth flexing, and grunted as she groped Tara's other fat tit.

Tara was embarrassed when she heard herself moaning. But the pleasure was stealing her breath, making her breasts heave, which only seemed to please Ohana further, for she grunted with arousal and sucked even deeper, harder, sometimes pulling her lips away with a smack and watching as Tara's tit wobbled, the nipple glistening wet.

Ohana looked down at Tara's face and seemed satisfied by her pink-cheeked arousal. Then the big woman leaned back on her knees, and as Tara watched in bewilderment, she spread Tara's thighs and pushed the hide skins up, exposing her sex. Then the white head bowed between her spread legs, and a moment later, Tara stared, unseeing, into space, as Ohana sucked and licked her sex, roughly tasting the lips, roughly and hungrily plunging her tongue.

Tara, thighs shaking, heard herself crying out, moaning, panting, screaming softly, screaming the names of the gods. And shivering with arousal, she suddenly understood why the other women had screamed. Ohana was very good at what she was doing. So, so good.

Grunting and moaning as she buried her face in Tara's sex, Ohana sucked on Tara's clit, then suddenly crammed two fingers deep inside, and Tara gasped and thrust her big breasts to the cave ceiling as she was roughly fingered to a hard climax.

· · · ·

AFTER THE FIRST TIME with Ohana, Tara was so exhausted that she slept straight through supper. As she lay beside the fire on her side, she was vaguely aware of Ohana and her family chatting and laughing as they ate. No one disturbed her, however, and she was even touched when one of Ohana's younger wives spread a blanket of deer hide over her.

It was the middle of the night and everyone was sleeping in the cave when Tara awoke with a start. Ohana's hard body was pressing against her in the dark, and the woman had placed a strong arm around her, trapping her in its hard embrace. She kissed Tara's neck without a word and groped at one of her heavy breasts.

Tara blushed a little and moaned, her clit immediately throbbing with desire. She felt Ohana's muscular leg hook behind her slender, shapely one and lift it – causing her loincloth to tumble back and reveal her sex. As she was groping Tara's big tit and kissing her neck, Ohana reached down and fingered roughly at her sex – so roughly, Tara's hips jerked, and she rocked on her side, big breasts jiggling as she gasped from the sudden pleasure.

Grunting with arousal as she watched Tara's jiggling breasts, Ohana fingered harder, faster, until Tara was panting shrilly and crying out. Ohana quickly covered her mouth, and kissing Tara's head, she kept roughly fingering, their bodies rocking, until Tara pressed her head back against Ohana and gave a muffled scream behind the warrior's hand as she helplessly came.

As if something had been achieved, Ohana let go, giving Tara a lazy kiss on the cheek and a slap on the backside that left her buttocks jiggling. The big woman then rolled over, and Tara lay there – panting and disheveled and undone, her breasts riding with her gasps, as the hard, hungry touch of the masculine woman lingered on her body.

And on it went every night. Tara would be sleeping peacefully, only to suddenly awake to the delicious thrust of Ohana's tongue in her sex, lips on her nipples, fingers inside her. The big woman came every night without a word and made rough love to her, groping and fingering and sucking, and she did not stop until Tara climaxed.

Sometimes Ohana kept going even as Tara was climaxing, forcing her to come again and again, and leaving her weak and undone.

The process was automatic every night, with Ohana growing more and more determined. And then, the first night Tara felt the flutter in her womb, she realized what Ohana had been after: Tara was pregnant. Somehow, because Ohana had fingered her, she was now carrying the woman's child.

Now Tara understood: with Ohana's child inside her, no other warriors would try to take her, leaving Ohana time to take care of her family without a constant threat looming over her shoulder. Tara, officially, had been claimed.

Tara still found it baffling, though. Why were the warriors of the clan so desperate to take her from Ohana? And why had Ohana insisted on taking her? One day, when she was out in the flower fields with Gar, she voiced her confusion and was met with laughter.

Gar was Ohana's fifth wife, a pretty young thing, very short, with big breasts heavy with milk and matted red hair. She was wearing a necklace of beads and bones as she sat across from Tara in the tall flowers, feeding her sixth child from one of her big breasts. She laughed when Tara voiced her confusion and looked at her with something like pity.

"What?" Tara demanded.

Gar shook her head. "Tara, you featherhead. You were the most beautiful unmated woman in the clan! Of *course* the warriors were stabbing each other over you!"

Tara cast her eyes down and blushed, embarrassed. She didn't feel like the most beautiful woman and was still amazed.

"Ohana is chieftess for a reason," went on Gar. "She always takes the biggest kill, the most territory, and the most beautiful women."

Gar started to speak again and hesitated, glancing around. They were not alone in the flower fields. There were many cave wives here, along with their giggling daughters. Anyone might have overheard them and spread gossip, but Tara wanted to hear what Gar had to say and damn the risk.

"What?" Tara begged. "Tell me!"

Gar bit her lip. "It's just . . . Now that you are with child, the warriors will move on to the next beautiful unmated – your sister."

Tara snorted. "What? Firga? She'll be a warrior, not a cave wife."

"No, not Firga," answered Gar heavily.

Tara laughed in disbelief. "You can't mean Marmar! She looks like a mammoth's ass. No one will want her."

Gar cast her eyes down. "No . . . not Marmar."

Tara paused in shock, mouth open. "What? Varg?! She's a child—!"

"And so were you only the season before," Gar somberly pointed out. "Now you've been claimed, and Varg is the most beautiful unmated in the clan. Of course, Ohana will wanted her." She hesitated and added, "Ohana has taken me and three of my sisters."

Tara sat stunned.

• • • •

TARA UNDERSTOOD HOW lucky she was to have been taken by the chieftess. Ohana was more than a worthy provider who took great care not only of Tara but of her mother and sisters as well. There was always plenty to eat, enough materials to make cooking utensils and clothes, and if the other warriors even thought about moving on one of Ohana's wives, she was more than willing and able to murder them.

And indeed, a few of the clan warriors were foolish enough to challenge Ohana for Tara even after she became with child. A few of them came to the cave shouting and boasting, and Tara watched in awe as big, strong Ohana casually cut them down. She mounted their heads on jagged rocks outside the cave, and after doing so, very few were foolish enough to try to take Tara.

Tara was protected, cared for, and greatly loved. Yes, loved. Ohana would look in her eyes as they were making love, and the big woman's eyes were so warm and soft with affection. Tara would never forget the first time they kissed. Somehow, sharing her wife with her sister was unthinkable, unbearable.

But more than once, Tara's mother and sisters came by the cave for supper. Suga was beside herself with delight that her daughter had been taken by the chieftess, and she often hugged Tara and wept for joy. Firga nodded solemnly in great approval, Marmar sulked in jealousy, and little Varg had fun playing with Ohana's daughters.

One night, sitting around the fire as everyone ate, laughed, and told stories, Tara couldn't help but notice how Ohana stared at Varg. As Gar had pointed out, Varg was fast becoming a woman, though she wasn't yet old enough to bare her breasts for a mate. Her little breasts, however, were blossoming behind her fur hides, and more than once, Tara had noticed Ohana gazing at Varg with flaring nostrils and a hard sort of hungry look.

One morning, Ohana held court outside her cave as she always did, sitting upon a great rock like a throne, knees spread, as the members of the Bear clan stood before her with their grievances. Tara was currently her favorite wife, and as such, she often sat on Ohana's knee as she held court. This day was like no other, and she sat on Ohana's knee as Ohana held Tara's waist in one arm, her eyes fixed on her supplicants.

The woman who currently stood before Ohana's "throne" was Sno, an older warrior woman with gray hair and hard, gray eyes. She was stiff and proud as she stood there, spear in hand, though she also seemed tired about the eyes. She lifted her chin as she said, "You *must* listen to me, Ohana. The Wolf clan is strong – too strong for even you. The only way we will survive is to appease them. We *must* send them women as a peace offering. Very beautiful women."

Ohana frowned irritably. She didn't like the sound of that. "Nonsense. Chieftess Turaga is a wild beast who will not be tamed with such feeble gestures. And even if I were to consider this groveling, who would I send? All the most beautiful women in the clan belong to me." So saying, she glanced down at Tara with soft affection, and Tara looked demurely down, her heart fluttering happily.

"And even if one of my daughters were old enough," went on Ohana dismissively, "I wouldn't dream of giving them to that beast."

"Ohana, something *must* be done," Sno grimly insisted, "or theWolf clan will come here and take our wives by force."

"I suppose it would ne prudent to appease the lunatic," Ohana bitterly relented, and Sno looked relieved.

Sitting on Ohana's knee with her big belly protruding, a sudden thought struck Tara. She cast her pale lashes down as she said slyly, "Ohana, my wife, I know just who you should send."

Varg couldn't believe how easily her mother had allowed her to be sold off to another clan, but Suga had seemed almost proud of what was happening! All the old woman could talk about was how her daughters would be rich and well taken care of while birthing mighty warriors and bringing fame to their once meager bloodline. She was so thrilled that the mightiest warriors were fighting over her daughters!

The rest of the family came out to see Varg off and seemed just as pleased as Suga. Firga told Varg that she should be proud of her beauty and to use it like a weapon, while Marmar sighed and told Varg she was so lucky to be so pretty. Varg thought that ugly Marmar, with her bristly unibrow and bucked teeth, and Firga, who would one day be a warrior in her own right, were the lucky ones. Neither of them would suffer the fate of being passed around like a prize!

Even Tara came to see Varg off, alongside her towering warrior wife. She kissed Varg on the forehead in farewell. Then she whispered so that no one else could hear, "The others won't understand. Such beauty is as much a curse as anything. The good warriors will want you, but so will the rapists."

Varg gasped in horror to hear this.

"Don't be afraid. Turaga is strong and will protect you. Take care, little sister," Tara said heavily.

Varg had no idea what they were on about. Her, pretty? She was not ready to be mated! Though she had bled and developed breasts, she felt like a child still. When she complained, Suga told her to hush and admitted that she had sheltered Varg for far too long. Varg was nearly twenty summers old!

Then three hard-eyed warriors from Clan Wolf appeared on the mountain trail – large, strong women wearing wolf teeth and gray fur hides—and Suga kissed Varg farewell and whispered to her that everything would be fine. Then one of the cold warriors stepped forward with rope, and Varg couldn't believe it when her hands and feet were tied!

A grim, big, burly warrior with flaming red hair gently lifted Varg around the hips and slung her across her shaggy horse like game, and as Varg was borne away down the mountain, she thought she saw Tara weeping into her hands with great shame. Suga put her arms around Tara to comfort her, which was a feat, for Tara was large with child.

Standing next to Tara as she wept, tall and towering Ohana put a comforting arm about Tara's shoulders, but the chieftess did not take her eyes from Varg, and they were hard with lust. Varg's heart skipped a shocked beat, and she thought she suddenly understood why she had been sent away. She could not escape the feeling that it had all been orchestrated by Tara out of jealousy and fear. But she could not hate her sister either. She might have done the same in Tara's place. What woman wanted to share her wife with her own sister?

As the horses bumped her along, Varg lay across the saddle on her belly, backside in the air, and wondered what Chieftess Turaga was like. Was she kind? Was she cruel? Would she beat Varg and hurt her?

. . . .

SUGA HAD TOLD VARG that the ride to the Wolf Clan camp would only take a couple days. Varg could feel the dread welling up inside her, and she hated being slung on her stomach across the shaggy horse. It was uncomfortable and she felt like a piece of meat. She wiggled a few times to get comfortable and instantly regretted it: her fur hides slid up, revealing her bare backside, her thighs, and the pink sex that bulged between with its fat lips.

The second she found herself exposed to the cold air, Varg felt the body of the red-haired warrior tense against her. The woman grunted softly with awkward arousal, and then – very slowly and discreetly, for fear of being seen by the others – she smoothed her big hand over Varg's soft backside and firmly squeezed.

Varg felt her clit throb at once in response and was embarrassed when she moaned softly. She bit her lip to stifle her cry, but she did not protest or show fear or anger. Instead, she glanced over her shoulder up at the big warrior woman, and her heart skipped gladly when she met her eye: the warrior was gazing down at her with hot hunger.

"Pretty little thing, baring your plump ass and tight pussy to me," whispered the redhead. "If Turaga finds out, she will kill me for having touched you. But it would be a worthy death."

Varg blushed a little and felt a thrill of happiness. There was something about this beautiful red-haired warrior, something strong and powerful – and yet gentle and soft.

As they continued slowly riding through the deep green forest, the redhead lingered in the rear, and with the others talking and laughing up ahead, she slowly and discreetly slid two big fingers between Varg's clenching thighs, through the heat and moisture of her sex.

Varg's lashes fluttered fast as she was filled, and her little pink lips parted as she gasped, frowning in bafflement. Then the warrior, gazing down at her with hard lust, began to finger her. It was deep and slow at first, then faster, harder, so that her elbow was jerking with the motion. She reached under as she was fingering and roughly ripped Varg's fur top open, exposing her jiggling breasts. Then she took one of Varg's fat tits in her fist and massaged it, fingering the nipple as she fingered her pussy deeper, faster, harder.

Varg lay across the horse, paralyzed with pleasure, gasping in rhythm as she was fingered, eyes staring blankly into space. She could feel the pleasure mounting and wiggled her hips against, which only excited the redhead, who fingered and groped her with renewed roughness and brutality, until she came with a helpless, choked cry.

Blushing, sex tingling from the rough pleasure, Varg sagged in delight across the horse again and was surprised when the redhead smoothed down her yellow hair with great affection and even gently pulled her fur hides down, covering her backside.

Varg's long yellow hair had tumbled forward in her face, and she was still panting and gasping as the redhead soothingly rubbed her back.

"Tight little virgin, never before touched. Would that I could take you from Turaga," the warrior said. "You are young and sweet and beautiful like no other. You should be First Clan Wife, but you will be Turaga's seventh, fucked and forgotten. Such a waste. At least I have taken your first pleasures for myself."

Varg was flustered and didn't know what to say. It pleased her to hear how desperately the red warrior wanted her, though. She was beginning to understand what Firga had meant by her beauty having power.

"I would kill Turaga and make you my woman, if you asked," said the redhead, shocking Varg.

Varg didn't answer. She wasn't clever and did not know how to scheme, and the thought of betraying Turaga frightened and confused her. She would much rather just submit and live her life without the drama, but as they continued to ride, the redhead kept whispering seductively, promising that she would feed Varg and care for her, protect her and love her. Varg had to admit she was flattered by the doting and blushed a little as she listened.

When dusk sent long shadows across the forest floor, the three warriors dismounted and made camp. The other two were big women with dark hair, one black, the other brown. They set about collecting firewood and building a fire, while the redhead seemed to be in charge of Varg. She gently slug Varg over her shoulder, carried her to the fire, and sat her on the dirt.

Varg's hands and ankles were still bound, so she nearly tumbled over but managed to remain kneeling, bound hands in her lap. One of her breasts was still exposed, and the cold hair made the pink nipple stand out hard from the swollen tit.

The three warriors sat around the fire, and Varg trembled a little with delight as they gazed at her. Their fierce, slanted eyes blazed with hunger, their lips were tight with it. They kept looking at her exposed tit, glancing over her narrow waist and round hips. Suddenly indeed proud of her beauty, Varg tossed her yellow hair back and lifted her chin. Would they fight over her? Already, Red Hair was irritated by the stares of the others.

"We all want to fuck her," said the redhead, shocking Varg. "So why don't we? It is better than killing each other over her."

"What will keep her from betraying us?" said Black Hair dismissively.

Red Hair waved a hand. "She is a hungry little thing," (Varg blushed hard) "and if she is smart, she will fear Turaga's anger."

The other two frowned at the fire, considering. Then Brown Hair lifted her eyes and said, "If we do this thing, we each shall swear on the gods to take it to the pyre."

"On the gods, I swear," said Black Hair.

"On the gods," agreed Red Hair.

Brown Hair nodded in approval. "On the gods, clan sisters. Who among us shall fuck her first? Let us cast lots."

Varg watched in silent amazement as the three warriors drew twigs from a pile. Black Hair drew the longest stick. Her dark eyes settled with satisfaction on Varg, who went still.

Black Hair was sitting on a rock, knees mannishly spread. She lurched up and stomped over to Varg, then knelt down behind her. Varg felt the woman gently grab a fistful of her hair, then she pulled, forcing Varg to lean back and thrust her big breasts forward.

Varg blushed when she understood what was happening. Her exposed tit lifted nicely as she was forced to tilt her body back, and now it jutted, plump and high, as if offering itself to be fondled and sucked.

Looking down over Varg's shoulder, Black Hair cupped her exposed tit from under and hefted it with appreciation. Then she squeezed and massaged, watching the pink nipple roll and harden in her grasp.

Varg's face was blazing hot, for the other warriors were watching as she was groped. They stared at her with glazed eyes, and their bodies were tense with desire. Deep down, Varg liked it. Her beauty tormented them, had driven them to betray their own chieftess! They would be killed if their actions were discovered!

Still groping Varg's tit, Black Hair leaned down and roughly kissed her on the mouth, tongue and all. Varg gulped on the kiss and felt her clit throbbing wildly. Then without warning, her bound ankles were grabbed, and she was roughly flipped on her back with a toss of her hair, breasts trembling.

Black Hair yanked a knife from her belt, and with her dark eyes blazing hunger, she cut Varg's ankles free and roughly snatched her thighs open in both hands. Looking down between her big breasts, Varg watched breathlessly as Black Hair's dark head bowed between her spread legs, and then she gasped, pretty eyes fluttering wide, as her fat pussy lips were sucked for the first time.

Black Hair was very good at what she was doing, was very passionate and eager, and she went about it sensual and slow, sucking in long sucks on Varg's pussy lips, then sucking hungrily on her throbbing clit, until Varg was gasping helplessly, her big breasts riding, as she stared at the stars above in baffled shock. The pleasure was too intense. She was embarrassed by her own shrill cries.

Head bowed between Varg's trembling thighs, Black Hair reached up and groped Varg's big tits as she sucked with slow hunger on her clit, and with her cheeks flaming, Varg thrust her big breasts to the stars and screamed softly as she came.

• • • •

VARG HAD SLEPT FOR perhaps an hour when she felt a beefy hand groping at her ankles. They were still unbound, and the beefy hand turned her over off her side and onto her back. Then two beefy hands closed on her ankles, and she screamed softly as she was dragged a few feet across the dirt. Her hips were easily lifted, her legs fell over someone's shoulders, and then a mouth was sucking with ravenous hunger on her sex.

Gasping from the pleasure, Varg looked down and saw Brown Hair's wild head moving between her thighs. The woman was clutching Varg's thighs to her shoulders, holding them in place, keeping her trapped as her pussy was so forcefully sucked. Had she wanted to escape, she could not have, and yet, the strength of the woman's burly arms thrilled her.

The sounds of sucking, slurping, and moaning soon rose against the gentle crackle of the fire, and then Varg was screaming softly as she came yet another time. Satisfied, Brown Hair looked down at Varg with hard lust, then gathered her up and carried her to the fire, where she sat on a rock with Varg in her lap.

To Varg's surprise, the other warriors were awake as well, and had been watching with narrowed, lusty eyes as Brown Hair ate Varg's pussy like a warthog. Now Brown Hair reached into a pouch on her rope belt, and pulling out a red berry, she pressed it in Varg's lips. Varg blushed a little – for the pressing of the woman's finger was suggestive – and she took the berries one by one into her mouth. She ate them a little eagerly, for they were delicious, and her belly was growling.

"That's right, pretty thing," Brown Hair said. "Eat these berries up, and your pussy will taste sweet."

Varg halted and blushed to her hairline in shock. The warriors chuckled around the fire.

"It's my turn now," Red Hair complained.

"No," said Brown Hair. "She shall kneel for me first."

The other warriors laughed at that, and Varg glanced at them in alarm, wondering what Brown Hair's words meant.

Brown Hair looked down at Varg with soft affection as she gripped the back of her neck and calmly ordered, "Kneel."

Lashes fluttering in confusion, Varg managed to clumsily slide off Brown Hair's lap and to her knees. She watched as Brown Hair hitched up her fur hides, revealing the sex between her hard thighs and how glossy it was with moisture. The hot, musky scent of it was arousing, and Varg felt her clit throb to life. Then Brown Hair, without a word, grabbed the back of Varg's head and pressed her mouth to her sex.

Varg froze in shock and heard the warriors laugh again.

"She has never knelt before," said Red Hair. "She will learn."

"Eat my pussy, girl," said Brown Hair softly.

Varg closed her eyes, inhaling the hot scent, enjoying the soft brush of the lips against her mouth, and suddenly, nothing in the world could seem more delightful. She sucked with her mouth, slid her tongue through the hot, wet, softness, and was proud of her skill when Brown Hair moaned.

To Varg's surprise, moisture suddenly squirted from her sex as she came, and she did not release her grip on Varg's head, instead holding her moutj against her.

Varg gave a muffled cry as she gulped the fluids, and when Brown Hair released her, she crawled feebly away, fumbling to hold herself up on her bound hands.

Laughter in the camp. Then without warning, Varg felt something thick and firm plunge hard in her pussy, forcing its brutal way through her heat and moisture. She screamed softly in shock and glanced back: Red Hair was wearing leather straps around her hips, and she was thrusting whatever was connected to it inside of Varg!

Without pausing, Red Hair began to thrust – so deep and hard that Varg rocked forward and back on hands and knees, her big breasts swinging, her buttocks jiggling as Red Hair slammed phallical object in. She stared into space through streams of yellow hair, gasping as she was rocked, and belong long, the pain became and afterthought as the pleasure took over.

Without warning, Red Hair pulled Varg back on her lap, and groping one pf Varg's big tits in her beefy fist, her other hand lifted Varg easily by the waist and slammed her down on the toy – pver and over until she screamed out in breathless ecstasy.

Varg's pussy was clenching on the toy now, and her clit was swollen and throbbing. Seeing this, Black Hair knelt down, and with narrow-eyed lust, she leaned forward anf sucked hungrily on Varg's clit as she was bounced. Brown Hair moved in and sucked one of Varg's big, jiggling tits, while Red Hair hotly kissed Varg's neck and groped her other tit. And as the three big, masculine women closed in on her, Varg gave a helpless, shrill cry and climaxed.

· · · ·

AS THE SUN WENT DOWN in the pink and purple sky, Turaga sat on a rock outside her tent, waiting for the three warriors to return with her new bride. In her hand was a spear woven with feathers, and on her head was a silver horned helm. She was in a bad mood, for the scouts had imparted to her some grim news, and when Scra, Magda, and Ufgar returned, they would be in for a world of pain.

Dagmar had tried to warn Turaga that the three rockheads could not be trusted, but since when did Turaga listen to her wives? Oh no. Turaga was the mightiest warrior in the land and knew everything!

Dagmar was First Wife and had been since she was nineteen summers old. Like the new bride, she had been given to Turaga as appeasement. For from the time she was very young, Turaga had been a capable warrior, a raider, and a conqueror, who the other clans feared. As a result, young women were constantly being sent to Turaga in order to quell her violence.

Dagmar had been one of the sheep people, one of many docile tribes that were always preyed upon by the barbarian brutes who roamed the forests. She still remembered her terrified mother offering her topless to Turaga, and how Tugara had taken one look at her tits and had agreed. And just like that, Dagmar's high breasts and tight pussy had bought peace and protection for her people, for Turaga still protected her clan even now.

Dagmar was a young and beautiful woman with long dark hair and great breasts. She sat on the grass beside Turaga, legs folded beneath her skirts, shoulders wrapped in a large and magnificent wolf-fur cloak, and bones adorning neck and dangling from her ears. Every now and then, she glanced sideways at Turaga while bitterly wishing she could be in bed. But Turaga had insisted she be there to greet the new bride.

Turaga's other six wives were inside the tent behind her, tending to the children, sewing, gossiping. They had been ordered to prepare the tent for the new bride's arrival, but Dagmar knew they were not. The other brides were lazy and spoiled and only did what Turaga told them if Dagmar was there breathing down their necks. They were likely lounging around half naked, forcing their smallest children to fan them with giant feathers, for while Turaga was a fierce warrior, she was often pushover with her wives and left the matter of commanding them to Dagmar.

The rest of the clan was watching for the new bride. They stood curiously in the mouths of their open tents, craning their necks to peer into the distance. Children giggled and asked loud questions and had to be shushed. Young wives put their heads together and whispered. Warriors stared into the distance with anticipation.

The arrival of a new wife for the chieftess was always an event in the Wolf clan. The warriors would make bets on how beautiful the new bride was, while the wives would make bets on how ugly. After all, there were clans who had the audacity to send Turaga ugly women – as a defiant rejection of her rulership or as a prank – and Turaga would immediately head out and eviscerate any clan that did so.

The Wolf Clan, after all, was quite powerful and nearly unstoppable, for it was many clans in one. Each clan Turaga conquered was given the option to join her clan or die. Dagmar's own clan had joined the Wolf clan. Her mother was in a tent just three tents down with her sheep wandering about outside it, their distant baas soft in the purple dusk.

"They come," said Turaga darkly. She was still seated straight and proud upon her rock and glared hard down the avenue between the tents, her spear in her strong fist.

Up the dirt path came the three fools: red-haired Scra, black-haired Magda, and brown-haired Ufgar. And walking between them, looking sheepish and guilty, was the new bride.

Dagmar's eyes danced over the young girl. She was small and pretty, with wide hips and big tits jiggling behind her skimpy fur hides. Her yellow hair was a long mess falling half in her frightened face, her ands were bond, and her head was down. She looked so guilty that Dagmar immediately knew what the scouts had reported was true: she had allowed Turaga's underlings to mate with her. The fool!

Dagmar shook her head and wondered how anyone could be so stupid. Why spread her legs for random warriors who barely had wives to boost of? Especially when she had the most powerful warrior in the Great Forest at her beck and call!

The little group stopped before Turaga where she sat, knees wide, upon the rock. They came forward, and the three warriors knelt down to show respect. As she was kneeling, Scra put her hand on the new bride's head and made her kneel as well.

The new bride trembled and bowed her head behind her yellow hair. She was terrified, and she should be, Dagmar knew, for Turaga was glaring down her nose at the girl with great dislike.

"Greetings, young wife. My scouts have told me that you fucked my warriors," Turaga said to the new bride, who sobbed and shook behind her hair, while either side of her, the three warriors stiffened in fear, their heads down.

"Is it true?" Turaga coldly demanded.

Dagmar heard the girl sniff, then she glanced up, eyes wet with fear, and stared at her knees again as she stammered, "It is t-true."

Turaga's nostrils flared and her breasts heaved in anger. Then without warning, her muscular arm snapped out, ramming her spear down through the top of Scra's head. Scra gave a choked cry as she was murdered, and her red blood spattered the new bride, who screeched in wide-eyed horror and scrambled sideways, falling over on her elbow. She stayed down, staring in open-mouthed horror as Turaga kicked Scra's squirting body off her spear in disgust.

Scra fell limply in the dirt and lay there, a pool of dark blood spreading around her. Then Turaga turned to Magda and Ufgar. Magda took her breath with dignity, lifting her chin and staring coldly into space, but Ufgar was a coward and leapt up to flee. As she was running, Turaga hurled her spear in disgust after her, and she collapsed facedown with the spear jutting from her back.

The new bride sat in the dirt and wept and wept, her soft gasps and screams of horror the only sound in the silence that followed. Everyone was watching, everyone was still. Dagmar herself sat very still, despite the blood that had hit her leg, and almost pitied the new bride. Almost. She was still, in the end, a stupid creature who brought Turaga's wrath down on herself.

Turaga stood over the new bride, muscular and strong, and sneered down at her in disgust. "Traitor," she hissed. "That you would allow those worthless nothings to pass you around! That you would spread your thighs for anyone else! Your thighs belong to me!" So saying, she grabbed a fistful of the weeping girl's hair and gently pulled, forcing her to stagger to her feet.

The new bride was terrified and frightened after the sudden violence—a sheltered little thing, Dagmar could tell – but she was also in awe of Turaga's strength and power. Several times, even as she was shaking and sobbing, she glanced up at Turaga with admiring eyes, bright and round, like a fascinated child. She began to sob absently, just staring at Turaga, who angrily ignored her silent doting.

Dagmar couldn't blame the little tramp. Turaga *was* a beautiful specimen, quite strong and commanding. Dagmar had been in awe of her as well. Sadly, while she was fond of Turaga, Dagmar had grown used to her by now. The new bride would be in awe of the chieftess for some weeks, perhaps a few months – just like the others – but then the infatuation phase would fade away, and the new bride would fall to the lazy content of lounging, gossiping, and weaving flowers in her hair, just like Turaga's wives did as pregnancy after pregnancy came. Just like Dagmar.

Still clutching a fistful of the new bride's yellow hair, Turaga pulled a knife from her belt. The girl stiffened in horror, but the chieftess only used it to cut the girl's wrists free. Then she cut at the new bride's fur hides, ripping and tearing them off, while the girl shivered and wept all the while. She was being striped naked before the entire clan, and many of the women watched with hard-eyed lust.

Big breasts shivering with her sobs, the new bride wept into her hands like a child. Turaga roughly took her by the shoulders and turned her around to face the clan. Then she roughly grabbed the new bride's thin little wrists and pulled them apart to expose her big breasts. Many zeroed in on them with lust.

The new bride blushed crimson and hiccuped with soft sobs as Turaga roughly cupped her breasts from behind and announced, "These tits belong to me!" Then Turaga reached down and hooked two fingers in the new bride's sex and jerked them, so that the new bride blushed with arousal and cried out in pleasant surprise. She blushed in shame and bowed her head as Turaga shouted, "This pussy belongs to me! She is *my* woman! She is mine to fuck! Mine to suck! Mine to touch! If one of you even *looks* at her wrong, you'll end up like Scra!"

Many glanced down at Scra's lifeless body, which was still pooling blood in the dirt. Darmar was amused by the fear in their eyes. The threat had been heard.

When it seemed her point had been made, Turaga grabbed a fistful of the new bride's yellow hair, yanked her head back, and kissed her roughly on the mouth, tongue and all. The new bride moaned with pleasure as she was so forcefully kissed, and Dagmar could see her struggling to gulp on Turaga's thrusting tongue. Her little pussy was already wet, and it dripped, leaving her thighs glossy as Turaga's fingers crammed roughly inside.

And as everyone watched, Turaga started to finger the new bride rhythmically, her fingers curling hard and fast in her pink little sex, so that the girl's hips jerked forward and back and her little cheeks blushed.

Turaga stopped kissing the girl, and eyes narrowed with satisfaction, she groped the girl's tit and fingered her pussy and watched with glazed lust as the girl gasped to a sudden climax. The new bride's pretty eyes fluttered wide in shock, and Dagmar knew what she was feeling: Turaga's seed had left her fingers and had rushed to fill the girl. Turaga had impregnated her before the entire clan in order to claim her.

Turaga let the new bride drop, panting and gasping, to her knees. The girl leaned forward, nearly fell, and caught herself on her hands. Her great breasts swung down, plump and swollen, the pink nipples hard. Her flat belly was heaving as she panted behind her tumbling yellow hair, and she knelt there on all fours, naked and beautiful, gasping shrilly to catch her breath.

"If you ever let another woman touch you again," said Turaga, glaring down at the new bride, "I will kill you." And with that, she turned and marched inside the tent.

As winter fell fast over the Great Forest, Tara gave birth to her first daughter, a tiny bundle of heat and giggles with a mop of curly white hair. All of Ohana's daughters had white hair. Every last one of them. The chieftess' genes were so dominant that many of her wives feared giving birth to a dark-haired child, for fear they would be accused of having strayed.

It was common for a warrior, let alone a chieftess, to murder a wife who had lain with another. Allowing a cave wife to wander was perceived as a weakness and could quickly destroy the reputation of the warrior. Sometimes, if the warrior knew who the wife had slept with, that other warrior was murdered instead. So long as blood was shed over the trespass, then the warrior's reputation remained intact.

Tara was confident that Ohana would never hurt her, even if she did stray. For it was quickly becoming common knowledge that Tara was quite simply Ohana's favorite. When the mighty Bear clan was ordered to head deeper into the Snowy Mountains for the winter, it was Tara who was allowed to ride before Ohana on her shaggy horse, with her little baby – Dagdag – cooing at her breasts. When Ohana made a good kill, it was Tara who was given the ripest meat. When Ohana returned from a raid bearing jewelry and hides, Tara was given the best dresses and bone necklaces. And every night, Tara was the first woman Ohana made love to.

Other, younger wives were taken by Ohana as the winter drew on, but always, Ohana came back to Tara in the dark of their cave and held her the night through as she slept.

Tara was in heaven. She had never dreamed that becoming a cave wife could be this wonderful, had never dreamed that the chieftess herself would want her. But looking back, Tara was starting to feel as if she should have known it would happen. For there had been many times when she was flowering that she had looked up and caught the chieftess eying her with quiet hunger. It had always startled and pleased her, though she hadn't known what to think of it.

One morning beside the mountain lake, all the cave wives were wading into the water with the children to bathe. Little girls were laughing and splashing, mothers washed their babies, and many young and nubile unmated stripped their curvy bodes bare and waded with swaying hips into the water. The warriors, meanwhile, kept watch on the parameter.

Tara had barely been eighteen at the time, old enough to be perceived as a woman by the warriors, but not yet old enough to claim. Young women were usually taken at nineteen or twenty, at the peak of their flowering, and Tara had been anticipating that day and wondering who would take her the next year.

Apparently, so had Ohana. For as Tara was bathing in the lake, she could feel eyes upon her, and when she looked up, Ohana was staring directly at her across the water. Tara remembered freezing in shock. Ohana had one of her tiny daughters riding her shoulders. The little girl was laughing, and Ohana was speaking to her absently, but her hungry eyes were fixed on Tara like a hot light.

Heart fluttering, Tara had leaned down, young breasts jiggling, and scooped water to her face. When she straightened up again, Ohana was still staring, eyes narrowed now with lust, and she did not look away. Blushing, Tara felt brazen enough to look right back as she caressed water over her breasts. She blushed harder when Ohana's nostrils flared with desire.

Ohana did not look away from Tara until one of her wives called. Then, very reluctantly, she turned away from Tara and toward her wife – the First Wife, Chuc'calla.

Tara remembered how Chuc'calla, realizing where Ohana had been staring, had glared across the lake at Tara. The First Wife had known even then that Ohana wanted Tara, even if Tara had been too foolish to realize it. And now that Tara was pregnant and they were living in the same cave, Chuc'calla was just as angry, just as seething, always watching with bitterness and spite as Tara was fawned over and adored.

Chuc'calla was a small woman with large breasts, wide hips, and quite a narrow waist after having birthed ten daughters for Ohana. She was in her late twenties, with slanted dark eyes and long, dark hair. Before she was chieftess, Ohana had stolen Chuc'calla from a rival clan, had made love to her, and had impregnated her so quickly, her original clan had no reason to steal her back – They could not have cared for Chuc'calla's child.

And so, the Elk clan submitted and joined the clan of the Cave Bear, falling into line for the sake of Chuc'calla, their princess, and for their own sake as well. After all, Chuc'calla had been glad to be stolen and had refused to return to her people, even ordering them to submit to the Cave Bear clan.

In those days, Chuc'calla was Ohana's favorite, though from the stories Tara had heard, it seemed as if Chuc'calla had been little more than a prize, proof that Ohana was strong and worthy of becoming the next chieftess.

Ohana's mighty father, the previous chieftess, had been on her deathbed at that time. Meanwhile, her many warrior daughters competed to take her place. By stealing Chuc'calla – the most beautiful woman in the Great Forest at the time – and forcing her clan to submit, Ohana had proven her worth.

Now Tara's children would fight with Chuc'calla's to one day take Ohana's place. Tara didn't want to think of that. She hoped that her daughters would be cave wives like her and stay out of any fighting.

Tara lay in the dark cave, on the soft fur hides, surrounded by Ohana's family, as the nearby fire crackled gently through the night. Many of Ohana's daughters were a few years behind Tara, teenagers who had grown into muscular warriors rather than cave wives. Already, they were violent and thirsty for sex, always staring at the pretty unmated women and boasting of which ones they would claim as wives. Ohana's oldest daughter with Chuc'calla – a girl named Targon – often complained that she had wanted Varg for herself.

Laying on her side as she cradled tiny Dagdag to her breasts, Tara looked across the sleeping women around her at Targon, who was sleeping peacefully on her back, white hair a glowing veil around her shoulders. Targon looked like a younger version of Ohana, white-haired and masculine and strong, muscular body wrapped in furs and leathers. She was beautiful, just like her father, and she seemed truly heartbroken that Varg had been sent away.

Tara felt guilty for that. Had she known that Targon wanted Varg, she would have suggested that Varg be given to her. Instead, she had convinced Ohana to send Varg far away to the Wolf clan, and all for her own foolish envy and pride!

Now Varg would have been miles and miles beyond reach, for the Wolf clan always headed further south during the winter, while following the shorter-haired mammoth herds. Even if Targon wanted to take Varg from Turaga, Varg was now too far away, and taking her would have started a clan war.

Ohana moaned as she came awake beside Tara. The chieftess turned on her side and threw a strong arm across Tara, pulling her close in a hard hug. Tara smiled as her head was kissed. Her blonde hair had grown out over the months, falling past her shoulders.

"What keeps you awake, Little Wife?" Ohana rasped, half-awake herself.

"It is cold, the fire is low," Tara lied. She did not want to tell Ohana the truth -—that she had manipulated her into sending Varg away, crushing Targon in the process, and that she now felt guilty.

"Mmm. Then I will keep you warm," Ohana whispered huskily in Tara's ear, and Tara felt her clit throb to life.

"Don't," complained Chuc'calla, who was laying on the other side of Ohana. "I am tired of listening to you fuck her! I am your First Wife! You should be fucking *me* every night!"

Chuc'calla sounded furious, but Ohana only chuckled softly. Then the chieftess sat up, revealing Chuc'calla, who was angrily lying on her back with her arms folded beneath her big breasts. Tara looked over and thought Chuc'calla achingly beautiful, with her dark hair and pretty eyes.

Ohana knelt over them both, resting back on her heels and looking down at them. She reached for their fur hide dresses and pulled them open, so that one of their breasts was exposed. Tara blushed as her big tit pushed free of the fabric, and so did Chuc'calla, who looked as if she was still trying to be angry but was distracted by Ohana's hungry staring.

Hard eyes glittering lust, Ohana took a tit in each hand and gently massaged, watching as the nipples hardened, watching as Tara and Chuc'calla both moaned and frowned against the pleasure. Tara could feel her clitoris pumping faster and harder and she knew the same was happening to Chuc'calla, who moaned helplessly when Ohana leaned down and sucked deeply on her tit.

Then Ohana leaned back again, and taking Tara's legs in both strong hands, she spread them and pulled them back, so that Tara's fur skirts slid up and her bent legs were open wide, revealing her pink sex. Tara looked over and couldn't believe it when she saw Chuc'calla glance furtively at her sex.

Then Ohana did something neither of them had anticipated: she pulled Chuc'calla up by the arm (Chuc'calla blinked in confusion) and clutching at the back of the First Wife's neck, she bent Chuc'calla forward, pressing her head between Tara's open thighs.

Tara gasped when Chuc'calla didn't hesitate but immediately started licking and sucking her pussy with passionate abandon. She gasped and moaned, mouth open in baffled shock, as Chuc'calla's hungry tongue fucked her to a sudden climax. As she was coming, Tara thrust her big breasts to the cave ceiling and cried out weakly, for fear she would wake her baby. But Dagdag stayed asleep in her arm, and almost immediately after she had come, Chuc'calla was between her legs again, sucking on her clit and fingering her so deliciously, Tara had to bite her lip to stifle the screams. She climaxed, red in the face, at least six more times.

When Tara lay there, spent and gasping, Chuc'calla kissed up her thighs, up her neck, and caught Tara's mouth to her own in a hungry kiss. Tara was shocked but kissed Chuc'calla back eagerly, glad for the feel of the woman's big, soft breasts against her own. They were kissing hungrily when Tara felt Ohana's warm lips sucking hard on her clit. Tara pulled her mouth free to scream softly, her pretty lashes fluttering, and as Chuc'calla showered her lips and neck with frantic kisses, Ohana ate Tara's pussy with such rough passion that she felt her sex clench and squirt against the woman's eager mouth.

• • • •

IT SEEMED THAT AFTER she was allowed to make love to Tara, Chuc'calla went from hating her to doting on her. When seated beside the fire in the evenings after supper, Chuc'calla would always find herself beside Tara, and she would kiss Tara's cheeks and braid her long yellow hair and dote on her, and woe to anyone who tried to hurt Tara's feelings! The other wives, observing that Tara was now Chuc'calla's favorite as well, fell in line, grudgingly respecting Tara and giving her a wide berth, least they stir the wrath of Chuc'calla!

Now, whenever Tara was sleeping at night, it was a toss between who would make love to her – Ohana or Chuc'calla? Sometimes it was just Ohana. Sometimes it was Chuc'calla. Sometimes it was both of them, pulling her dress up to suck her tits and kiss hungrily at her mouth, tongues thrusting.

Sometimes, Tara awoke in the night and could hear Ohana making love to Chuc'calla. She would look over and blush brightly to see Chuc'calla squatting on Ohana's face, head back in ecstasy, while Ohana clutched her backside in plump fistfuls to hold her up.

Chuc'calla would twist her hips, grinding her pussy on Ohana's tongue until she came.

One night, Chuc'calla sat on Ohana's face in the opposite direction, so that she was facing away from her. She leaned forward as Ohana ate her out, hands bracing on Ohana's rippling belly, big breasts jiggling as they poured from her fur tunic, and as she sighed and rode her wife's face . . . she would look across at Tara and smile lustily. Tara would blush deeply and return to sleep.

Yet another night, after Ohana and Chuc'calla had sucked Tara's tits and ate her pussy – both of them at the same time—Chuc'calla introduced Tara to what she called Ohana's "spear." It was a sex toy made of sheep skin, shaped to resemble an animal's erect phallus. Straps were connected to it, and when Chuc'calla strapped the toy to Ohana's hips, the phallus stood erect from her pelvis.

Without hesitating, Ohana looked at Tara with glazed lust, then grabbed Tara by the hair and turned her around. Heart pounding, Tara looked quickly at Chuc'calla when the First Wife took her baby. On her knees in the dark, she didn't understand what was happening until the phallus crammed hard and fast through the heat and moisture of her wet pussy.

Tara gasped, eyes fluttering wide, then hooding as the phallus filled her. She was still upright on her knees, and Ohana hooked a hard arm around her waist, just beneath her big tits, which sat on the warrior's arm as if offering themselves to be sucked. Then Ohana started pounding the "spear" in – deep, hard – and Tara rocked on her knees, trapped in the big woman's arm, and gasping as her tits jiggled.

Tara could feel the pleasure throbbing in her sex as she was pounded, and before long, she was so weak from the pleasure that she could barely hold herself up. Yellow hair half in her face, she glanced over in a daze of pleasure and saw Chuc'calla. The First Wife was cradling Dagdag in her arms, but her pretty eyes were narrowed on Tara's big tits as they jiggled from Ohana's hard thrusting.

Ohana slammed her hips against Tara again, forcing her soft backside to jiggle, driving the fake phallus in hard, and as Tara cried out shrilly, her tits jiggled wildly yet again. Ohana groped one of them, massaging it smoothly in her fingers, so that the pink nipple rolled, and unable to stand simply watching much longer, Chuc'calla leaned forward and sucked Tara's tit as she was fucked.

• • • •

TARA DIDN'T KNOW WHAT to tell her mother. Suga asked often if she was happy, and she was, but she wondered what would happen if it was discovered that the First Wife was going down on her each night. She had never heard of cave wives pleasuring each other without punishment, for that right belonged to the warrior wife alone. It was almost as if Ohana had elevated Chuc'calla's status, giving her a privilege no First Wife had ever been given before.

For the first time, Tara understood just how deeply Ohana loved Chuc'calla. She probably would have given the First Wife the moon if she had asked. Instead, Chuc'calla had asked for Tara! That's what all the hatred and envy had been about. Chuc'calla was not jealous of Tara having Ohana's attention but the other way around.

Tara supposed she didn't mind. It was cute and sweet, Chuc'calla's affection and desire for her. They just had to keep it a secret, for cave wives touching each other was strictly frowned upon, and Ohana would be perceived as weak and possibly exiled if it were discovered that she allowed her wives to lay together.

And so, it became a rule that Tara and Chuc'calla would never lay together without Ohana. But Chuc'calla's brazen desire for Tara only seemed to escalate. One night, as Ohana was sleeping, Chuc'calla crawled over to Tara, and laying down beside her, she kissed Tara on the mouth. Tara awoke with a start but happily kissed back. When she opened her eyes, however, Ohana was still sleeping. Chuc'calla had touched her alone.

"Are you crazy?" Tara hissed. "We can not touch without Ohana!"

Tara's heart fluttered when Chuc'calla touched her cheek with the back of her fingers, and her eyes were warm with love as she said helplessly, "I thought of you all day. I think of you all night. I want you for myself. I do not wish to share you with Ohana."

Tara stared back at Chuc'calla in shock.

"I love you!" Chuc'calla whispered desperately.

Tara blushed a little. "Chu . . ." she started in confusion, but her words were halted when Chuc'calla suddenly kissed her. Tara melted. Chuc'calla was a wonderful kisser, and her tongue thrust warm and strong against Tara's. Tara moaned and kissed her back, thinking to hell with it. To hell with the world. If she was honest, she loved being with Chuc'calla as well. She had come to love it even more than being with Ohana.

Happy that Tara had given in, Chuc'calla kissed down her neck, to her breasts. She paused and pried one of Tara's big tits from her fur tunic, then gave the pink nipple a slow suck. Tara moaned, reaching up to cradle Chuc'calla's head to her breasts. But Chuc'calla kept kissing down and down until she came to Tara's thighs. She paused, smiling with helpless affection at Tara, before spreading her thighs and bowing her dark head between.

Tara gasped on her back, big breasts heaving, as Chuc'calla's hungry lips and tongue pleasured her. Chuc'calla loved thrusting her tongue inside, sometimes pausing to suck with wet lips on Tara's clit. She moaned as she tasted Tara's pussy, her soft cries of desire rising with Tara's shrill gasps of delight. Then she slid her tongue as deep as it would go, plunging it through the tight walls of Tara's sex, and as she tongue-fucked Tara deeply, Chuc'calla reached up and massaged her big tits in both hands.

Frowning in baffled delight, Tara thrust her big breasts against Chuc'calla's caressing hands, and she was about to come when she felt Chuc'calla's mouth and hands suddenly ripped away. Chuc'calla screamed softly, then begged in a sobbing voice. There was a smack and a scream. Had Chuc'calla been stricken?

Heart pounding, Tara sat up on her elbow and froze in horror: Ohana had awoken – as well as three of her other wives – and to save face, she had grabbed Chuc'calla by the hair and had pried the First Wife off of Tara. With tight lips, the chieftess threw Chuc'calla to the floor, where the First Wife lay on her side, leaning on her elbow, her head bowed behind her dark hair. Chuc'calla's shoulders were shaking and she was weeping, but why? Surely Ohana wouldn't hurt them!

Tara met eyes with Ohana and her heart shrank with fear: the chieftess was glaring at her, tight-lipped and furious. She gathered little Dagdag from the furs and into her arms, glaring at Tara all the while, and without looking away from Tara, she handed the baby off to one of her frightened wives. It was Gar. The baby awoke and began to scream in Gar's arms, and the redhead tried to shush it.

More and more of Ohana's wives and daughters were waking now. They sat up, sleepy and rubbing their eyes, gasping in shock to see Chuc'calla weeping and Tara sitting there with her fur dress hiked up.

Tara's heart was pounding in fear. She had never before seen Ohana so angry! The chieftess grabbed her by the hair and dragged her to her feet. The motion was rough and angry, forcing Tara to bend over sideways, barely able to see for the hair in her face. Her scalp burned with pain from Ohana's yanking, and she wept softly, but she refused to beg.

Ohana had never before been so rough and cruel! Tara heard Chuc'calla screaming and begging, then she could see the woman's little feet as she, too, was snatched up by the hair.

Then Ohana stomped toward the mouth of the cave, toward the starry winter night, and Tara and Chuc'calla were forced to follow on hasty feet as they were pulled along by the hair, bent forward and half-blind. Behind them, Ohana's family asked what was happening, and Chuc'calla's children screamed for their mother.

Tara was suddenly grateful little Dagdag was too young to remember this. She did not want her daughter to remember how her mother had been banished. She did not want Ohana to be remembered that way, as a tyrant, for Tara didn't hate Ohana, even in that heartrending moment, she loved her.

With an angry grunt, Ohana shoved Tara and Chuc'calla out of the warm firelit cave and into the dark and the cold. They fell hard in the snow, and Tara cut her arm on a rock. She sat up, weeping in pain, and was touched when Chuc'calla put an comforting arm around her and kissed her cheek. Seeing this, Ohana's body tensed with anger, for they were embarrassing her further with her brazen affection: having heard the noise, many warriors and their wives were gathering at the mouths of their caves to watch.

"Go," Ohana coldly to them, "and never return on pain of death."

Tara's mouth fell open. She couldn't believe what was happening. She scowled. "Give me my baby! Give me Dagdag!"

"You will never see Dagdag again," Ohana answered. "I will not even tell her the name of her traitor mother."

Tara's breasts heaved in anger. "GIVE ME MY BABY!" she defiantly hurled.

Tara screamed softly in shock when Ohana picked up a rock and lifted it as if she would throw it. She cringed in Chuc'calla's arms, and Chuc'calla hugged her protectively as she whispered, "Come! We must go – or Ohana will be forced to kill us!"

Tara didn't want to leave Dagdag behind, but one look in Ohana's eyes told her that she had little choice. She allowed Chuc'calla to help her stand, and as they held each other and staggered down the snowy mountain trail, the rest of the Cave Bear Clan shouted and hurled stones at them. They were hit only a few times, but the longer they walked, the more numb Tara became. Until it was like walking through snowfall.

· · · ·

LIFE IN THE GREAT FOREST without warriors to protect and provide was hard for Tara and Chuc'calla. Chuc'calla was smaller and weaker, and so, Tara decided to take up the role of hunter and provider. At dawn, she headed out to begin the clumsy task of fishing and hunting, later returning at night to their cave deep in dark forest. Sometimes she caught nothing, and Chuc'calla would smile through her tears and comfort her that they would be fine somehow.

Without Dagdag to drink her mother's milk, Tara's breasts became heavy with it. Chuc'calla took to drinking her breast milk, sucking tenderly on her tits at night as she lovingly fingered her to a climax.

Tara was always relieved when her beasts became lighter, but the next day, they were heavy and dripping again, which made it harder to hunt. It became almost routine that Chuc'calla would suck her heavy tits like a hungry babe, sucking the milk sweetly away as she held her close and caressed the swath of hair about her pussy.

The nights were hard and cold. They held each other beside their little fire to keep warm. Sometimes warriors came close as they were hunting, and frightened they would be discovered, Tara and Chuc'calla retreated deep into their cave. The warriors never bothered to search the cave, however, believing there might have been a saber cat inside, and so, Tara and Chuc'calla slipped by easily enough that winter.

The winters were always long in the Age of the Bear, when the bear constellation rose high in the sky. The winter lasted eighteen years. Eighteen years of hunting and fishing and fucking and kissing there in the deepest depths of the Great Forest. And then one day, as the first ice melted, Tara caught her reflection in the water's mirror and realized she had aged.

Tara was almost forty. There were lines under her eyes and her once perky breasts were lower. And she had changed – had changed so that she could care for Chuc'calla. Her body was more muscular and she had cut her yellow hair short, and her eyes were hard from long years of suffering in the cold. She missed her baby. She missed Dagdag, and she realized with a pang that her daughter would have been claimed by a warrior by now.

"How time flies," said Chuc'calla wistfully. She stood in the mouth of the cave beside Tara, and their arms were lovingly interlocked as they watched the dawn blossoming pink and orange through the trees.

Tara looked at Chuc'calla and knew that she loved her. Chuc'calla had been a wonderful partner over the years, always so devoted to Tara's happiness. How many warm nights did they spend, cuddled together beside the fire and simply enjoying the warmth of each other's embrace?

Chu"calla had aged gracefully. Her big breasts were lower and there were lines around her eyes, her black hair was streaked with gray, and somehow, all of it made her seem quite beautiful and regal and strong, like an ancient tree. But she was sad, as well. She missed her daughters as much as Tara missed Dagdag.

"If we returned now, would our children recognize us?" Chuc'calla wondered, an unshed tear gathering in her eye.

Tara didn't know what to say, how to comfort Chuc'calla, so she kissed the shorter woman on the cheek and put her arm around Chuc'calla's shoulders.

Chuc'calla smiled at this affection. "I still love you, Tara," she said, startling Tara into looking at her again. "After all these years, I love you . . . with every breath in my body."

Smiling, Tara turned to face Chuc'calla, and they were silhouetted against the rising run as she bent Chuc'calla back in a passionate kiss.

Varg was surprised, but she was actually glad she had been traded away to the Wolf clan. She missed her mother, her friends, and her sisters, but Turaga's wives were just as kind and warm, comforting her and welcoming her, and the First Clan Wife, Dagmar, was very much like a mother – though much more stern than Suga had ever been.

Dagmar took Varg aside and scolded her for betraying the chieftess with other women. She explained – sternly and yet somehow gently and patiently – that Turaga was a very short-tempered woman who would put up with no nonsense. If Varg messed up again, she might be the one to take a spear, not her lover.

Dagmar seemed very adamant about what she was saying and also seemed very worried for Varg, who she often called "foolish young one." The end result was that Varg lived in great fear and lust of Turaga. For the chieftess was beautiful and powerful and incredible in bed – but she was also terrifying, dark, cold.

When Turaga laid with Varg, there was no tenderness or affection. She did not kiss Varg unless it was her thighs or neck. The big masculine woman was rough and demanding, spreading Varg's thighs as she was sleeping and holding them apart in her hard hands, before bowing her head and eating Varg out ravenously.

It wasn't uncommon for Varg to be sleeping in the tent between Turaga and Dagmar only to be awoken by Turaga groping her tits and sucking, fingering her pussy and biting her neck. It was all night, every night, and Varg was in shock and ecstasy. She had never known such rough, relentless pleasure and was embarrassed by her shrill cries as the chieftess fingered her to a hard climax.

Varg was so happy, she found herself giggling and smiling for no reason. She was clearly the favorite of the chieftess, doted upon even more than Dagmar herself. Everywhere Turaga went, she took Varg with her. She even took Varg hunting with her, letting Varg ride before her on the shaggy horse with her tits bouncing. And with the rest of the hunting party watching, Turaga would finger Varg and grope her exposed tits right there on the horse, until she cried out Turaga's name as she came.

The other warriors were jealous. Incredibly jealous. They watched Varg with hungry eyes and darted glares at Turaga when her back was turned. The bolder ones likely would have tried to take Varg against her will or perhaps even seduce her, except Turaga took Varg everywhere and always had a hand around her wrist in a vice grip. When they were seated at the giant camp fire, Varg sat in Turaga's lap with the woman's hard arm around her narrow waist, so that her tits sat plump and bare upon it. And when they slept at night, Varg was always directly beside Turaga on the furs, cuddles tight in her hard, muscular arms.

Turaga's paranoia and jealousy went for months, until one day, Varg's belly began to show, making it clear that she was with child and had officially been claimed. The other warriors sullenly backed down, but Turaga did not take her eye off of Varg. Now she had to protect not only Varg but their child as well. She was grim and near frantic.

Varg didn't understand why. Turaga had more than ten wives and more than twenty children. What was Varg and her child? They were just more mouths to feed in the coming long winter. And yet, Turaga was focused almost exclusively on Varg. When Varg was too big with child to ride a horse, Turaga would return from the hunt, remove her horned helm, and immediately start going down on Varg – as of to prove that she was the still the best lover in the entire Great Forest.

And, oh, she *was*. The sound of Varg's breathless cries as she climaxed soon became as regular as the sun setting through the trees each day.

When the first snows began to fall, the clan packed up and began the journey south, following the short-haired mammoth herds to the warmer climates. There would still be snow further south, but unlike the Bear clan, the Wolf clan preferred lighter drifts.

Varg was placed in the back of a cart, which was pulled by an old shaggy horse, and then the great Wolf clan began the journey south, sometimes stopping to make camp at night, sometimes not stopping at all.

They came at last to a place known as the Ancient Grove, where pillars of stone stood with ancient carvings on them. There was a waterfall that had frozen over crystal blue, and the trees here reached their naked branches to the gray sky.

They made camp in the center of a circle of stones, upon an ancient burial mound. Varg thought that was strange, but Turaga insisted it was not. The chieftess then proceeded to explain a prophesy given by a witch, in which her youngest child would be born in the home of the ancients, upon their bones, and said child would rule the Great Forest.

Turaga then stared meaningfully at Varg, who stared back and did not know what to say.

Witches could not be trusted. In fact, a sensible person chopped off their heads! But here Turaga was, speaking of prophesies and nonsense! Varg couldn't believe it! But she didn't want to hurt Turaga's feelings, so she kept her mouth shut and smiled and agreed that their baby would one day rule the Great Forest.

Three months into winter, and the baby was born. Varg happily fed the baby girl from her heavy breasts and named her Frigg. Turaga looked on in pride and nodded in agreement as they sat around the great fire together, smiling at their child as it drank from its mother's breasts.

Frigg looked a great deal like Turaga. She had the same eyes and the same long, dark brown hair. She would grow to be a warrior. At least, Turaga was certain of it.

The winter lasted until little Frigg was walking on chubby legs. That bright and chilly morning, Varg sat on Turaga's lap as the chieftess held court in the circle of stones. The chieftess was sitting upon a big rock, one arm around Varg, as she listened to one of her warriors speak. The snow was melting and the first grass was pushing through, butterflies were already floating over the camp, and Frigg ran after them with one of her older half-sisters, squealing and clapping her hands.

Just then, a scout returned to their great camp and announced that Chieftess Ohana had cast out her wife, the yellow-haired Tara, for betraying her with another cave wife.

Sitting on Turaga's lap, Varg listened to the scout in horror. If Tara had been cast out, then there was no more reason to uphold the alliance between Bear and Wolf. Turaga could move on the clan and take it if she wanted to.

Chieftess Turaga seemed quite pleased by the news and sat up straighter as she listened. If she was going to strike, now was the perfect time. The Bear clan would be low on supplies just after the long winter, they would be weak.

"We must move, and quickly," said the scout, who sounded as excited as Turaga looked.

Turaga maintained a cold visage, but Varg could tell her wife was eager to take the Bear clan. She had spoken of nothing else for months. Varg twisted around and placed a pleading hand on Turaga's muscly arm, gazing up at her with wide eyes.

"Please, my wife," Varg begged. "My mother and sisters are still with the Bear clan—"

Turaga cupped Varg's face and peered down at her with a startling amount of affection. Then she looked past Varg as if she had not spoken and commanded the scout, "Go and find Morgar, my second—"

"Yes, chieftess—"

"And order the clan to pack up. We move tonight."

"Yes, cheiftess!"

Varg burst into tears as the scout took off running and dropped her face in her hands. After a pause, she felt Turaga's gentle hand stroking her long, yellow hair. The chieftess leaned forward and whispered soothingly, "Your family will be captured unharmed – unless they choose to fight back. I shall care for your mother, bring Firga into my warriors, and Marmar – I shall find her a fine warrior to mate. I shall take care of them."

Varg's sniffles quieted. Turaga's voice was so soothing, she didn't know what to think. Perhaps everything would be fine. And she was excited by the prospect of her family joining the Wolf clan.

. . . .

THE WOLF CLAN PACKED and began the journey back north. At the great oak tree, many of the warriors parted ways for the raid, led by Chieftess Turaga, who sat straight and cold upon her shaggy horse. Less than half of the warriors remained to guard the clan, and the raiding party was gone.

Before she left, Turaga kissed Dagmar dotingly on the lips, and then – surprising Varg completely – she yanked Varg close and kissed her tenderly on the mouth, then patted little Frigg's head and smiled at her. After that, Turaga mounted her shaggy horse and rode away, without looking back at her gathered wives and weeping children.

Days went by at the new camp, then months, and Varg slowly began to realize Turaga was not coming back. She sat in the tent with Dagmar and the other wives, sadly cradling her child to her breasts, and there were some nights where they barely spoke, barely slept for their sadness.

Then early one morning, there was the sound of a horn, and through the misty dawn there came riding warriors of the Bear clan. Varg looked out the tent and her heart dropped, for she recognized them! They had defeated Turaga – these same young women she had grown up alongside her murdered her wife! – and now, the remaining warriors of the Wolf clan rode out to meet them.

Varg couldn't look. She already knew what would happen. There were just too many warriors from the Bear clan. They were outnumbered. They would be taken and forced to join the Bear clan – which Varg found oddly terrifying, since they were her original clan. Perhaps they would treat her kindly, knowing she was one of them.

The clash of axes and shields rang in the pale dawn, the sounds of warrior screams pierced the air. Then there was panting and cries of pain as fallen warriors were suddenly brought the mercy of a quick death. Boots stomping in the snow, and then the sound of screams as the cave wives were taken.

Varg closed her eyes and hugged Frigg tight to her chest as more boots stomped toward the tent where she and Turaga's other wives hid. The tent flap was ripped open to reveal several leering warriors, and then there was complete chaos as the Bear clan warriors lunged inside and started snatching women.

The women scattered. Some were tossed over shoulders, others fought back and were smacked to the ground, others were grabbed by the hair, while their children clung to them and screamed. Dagmar sat very serene and still in the midst of the chaos, legs folded, and when a young warrior demanded that she rise, she obeyed and was roughly flipped over the young warrior's shoulder and carried away like a prize.

Horrified, Varg clutched her baby to her breasts and ran out into the snow, yellow hair streaming. Blinded by tears, she ran smack into someone and fell hard on her backside, managing to keep little Frigg tight in her arms. Frigg screamed and screamed in fear, and Varg kissed her daughter's head and tried to shush her.

"I will take you," said a voice, "but not my enemy's child."

Varg slowly looked up and went still: Chieftess Ohana was standing over her. The white-haired woman was so big, she was blocking out the sun. A stripe of dark war paint was across her eyes, making her look fierce and cold as she peered down at little Varg where she cringed in the grass.

Varg shivered under the woman's lusty stare and felt guilty when her clitoris stated to throb, but she had always secretly desired Chieftess

Ohana. She suspected it was the reason Tara had conspired to send her away. Now Tara was the one living in exile, and Varg was about to be claimed by the mighty chieftess of the Bear clan. Varg had never before held any resentment toward her sister, but some small part of her felt Tara had gotten exactly what she'd deserved.

Behind Ohana, women from the Wolf clan were being carried away, kicking and screaming, breasts jiggling. One woman was running and sobbing as a warrior laughed and chased her. The warrior caught up, grabbing the back of the woman's fur dress, which tore down her front, causing her breasts to shiver free. The woman screamed and covered her breasts as she staggered to a horrified stop. The warrior was on her in a heartbeat, groping her breasts from behind and kissing her neck. Varg was shocked when the woman's sobs quieted to moans of pleasure. The warrior started fingering her pussy right there, as other warriors gathered to hoot and watch, femme cave wives kicking on their shoulders.

"Drop the child," said Ohana in a low, steely voice.

Varg tightened her hold on little Frigg, who kept screaming, red-faced from fear. "No!" Varg sobbed.

"We want only the young and fertile. We are not taking the old women and the children," said Ohana. "The child will stay here with them. It will be taken care of. There is goat milk for the babes—"

"No!" Varg snapped, eyes blazing. She felt a sense of satisfaction when Ohana was shocked by this. Apparently, no feminine woman had ever disobeyed her before – Well, before Tara. Perhaps Varg and Tara were more alike than Varg cared to admit.

Lips tight, Ohana leaned down and grabbed little Frigg by the scruff of the neck, prying her away. She gently dropped Frigg on the ground, where the child sat screaming and crying, and then, eyes blazing lust, she grabbed Varg by the hair and yanked her to her feet.

Varg screamed and twisted, trying to get back to Frigg. She broke free and lunged forward, but Chieftess Ohana grabbed her from behind, locking little Varg in her hard arms. Varg kept twisting and calling Frigg's name, and Ohana ignored her struggling, instead grabbing a fistful of her fur dress and roughly ripping the front open. Varg sobbed as one of her big breasts bounced free, and then Ohana was cupping it and massaging it, gliding her finger over the hard pink nipple. She gently kissed Varg's neck as she cupped her milk-heavy tit, squeezing and massaging until a bead of milk dripped free.

Varg fell still and was ashamed of herself when her clit started to throb afresh. But how long had she wanted Ohana, this big and powerful woman, for herself? Now it had finally happened, and she could feel her sex throbbing as it filled with blood.

"Perfect tits," Ohana whispered, "and now they're mine. Your tits and your little pussy." And so saying, she reached down between Varg's thighs and crammed two fingers in her sex. Varg blushed hard when the woman's fingers slid in easily, when her sex reacted by tightening in delight. She squeezed her thighs on Ohana's insistent hand and moaned as she was fingered deeply, yet gently, until the moisture was sliding down her thighs.

Gently fingering Varg's pussy, Ohana kissed Varg's neck, cupped her face, looked at her with soft affection, and cupped her heavy tit. She grabbed Varg's face without warning, and forcing Varg to turn her head and look up at her, she kissed Varg hungrily on the mouth.

Varg's felt her pussy tighten and squirt over Ohana's deeply stroking fingers as she cried out and helplessly surrendered.

· · · ·

VARG HATED LEAVING her daughter behind, but she told herself that Frigg would be taken care of. Cave wives were often passed from warrior to warrior, for raids happened often, and children were lost in the chaos. Such was the way of the Great Forest – and whatever lay beyond once the Nordic clans had mastered the sea.

The ride back to Clan Bear territory was only a few days. In that time, Varg rode before Ohana on her shaggy horse, moaning whenever the woman groped her and feeling guilty for her pleasure. She thought often of Frigg and wept gently, wishing she could have brought her child along. Seeing this, Ohana promised her many strong children who would grow to be great warriors and beautiful cave wives, but Varg wanted Frigg.

At the Snowy Mountains, Ohana dismounted outside a cave, gently slung Varg over her shoulder, and carried her inside the dark entrance. They were immediately swamped by cave wives and small children, all of them bright and eager and asking questions. Ohana's little daughters asked her for presents, while Ohana's wives dotingly kissed her cheeks and wiped her hair clean of blood. One wife even took Ohana's axe for her and struggled to set the heavy thing aside with her shield.

Ohana only smiled at her family in greeting, but she answered no one. Instead, she set Varg on her feet, then called for someone to come forward. "Dagdag!" she called.

A second later, and a small child with white hair had waddled forward through the parting crowd. Varg's heart softened when she saw the girl, for she was about the same age as Frigg, barely one year. She gazed up at Ohana with big blue eyes from behind a swath of messy white hair, and when she smiled, her eyes crinkled up. "Father!" the child squealed happily.

Ohana smiled with soft affection down at the tiny girl. "I have brought a mother for you," she said to the child, and so saying, she picked little Dagdag up (Dagdag kicked and giggled) and dropped her in Varg's shocked arms.

"Mother!" Dagdag cried and immediately sucked upon one of Varg's milk-heavy breasts.

Varg looked down at Dagdag with soft affection, her heart warming as the child quietly suckled in her arms.

Ohana turned to Varg and touched an affectionate hand to her cheek. "She will not replace the other," Ohana said, referencing Frigg, "but she is yours now. She is your niece and now your daughter."

Varg's heart skipped a shocked beat when she realized exactly who Dagdag belonged to. Before she could speak, Ohana turned away.

• • • •

LATER THAT NIGHT, AS the fire crackled low in the dark cave, Varg lay on her side in the furs as Ohana's family slept around her, and she wondered how Tara could have been so stupid as to lay with another cave wife. Tara had been the favorite of Ohana, had been pampered and spoiled, and she had given it all up for what? A moment's pleasure?

But Varg had to suppose that she was little more than a hypocrite for criticizing her sister. After all, she had lain with low-ranking warriors on a whim, before she'd even met Turaga, and had gotten them all killed in the process. She was no better than Tara, really.

But perhaps it was deeper than that. Perhaps Tara had truly loved the woman she had betrayed Ohana for. Varg knew she would never know either way. Tara had been exiled and would never be seen again on pain of death.

And what was Varg to tell little Dagdag when she grew up? That her mother was a traitor? It would make Tara and Ohana both look bad, but then again, perhaps they deserved to look bad.

Little Dagdag was curled against Varg in the furs, and Varg was stroking the child's soft white hair, when she felt a strong hand grip her ankle and flip her easily onto her back. Varg cried out softly, big breasts trembling as she landed gently in the nest of her long yellow hair.

Ohana was hovering over Varg, eyes narrowed and glittering with lust in the firelight. She yanked Varg's already-torn fur dress open, forcing her big tits to bounce free, and then groped and massaged them in rough hands. The nipples were rock hard and beading milk.

Ohana squeezed them, watched the milk bead, and leaned down to suck gently.

Varg moaned and cradled Ohana's head to her breasts. The chieftess approved of this, leaning up to kiss Varg tenderly on the lips. Varg's heart fluttered happily at this affection, and she was pleased by the warm look in Ohana's eye. All of this doting and desire and affection – and Tara had given it up for what?

Then the chieftess pushed up Varg's dress, pushed it up so that it was rumpled over her breasts, leaving them to poke from under it and leaving Varg's curvy young body exposed to the cold air. Her eyes softened as she kissed down Varg's trembling belly, and Varg felt her clit throb. She knew what Ohana had come for and submissively spread her thighs: Ohana wanted to officially claim her by making her big with child.

Pleased by Varg's submission, Ohana kissed her thighs. Then the chieftess bowed her head between and sucked long and slow on her clitoris. Varg moaned as the pleasure flushed through her. Ohana was just as good as Turaga, perhaps better.

Varg's lashes fluttered and she gasped, staring in shock at the cave ceiling as Ohana sucked and licked her pussy until it was dripping. Then Ohana's fingers slid inside – slowly, deeply plunging through the tight walls of her heaving sex – and Varg moaned and melted into the furs as she was slowly fingered and sucked to a weak climax. Her thighs trembled and she jerked her hips, wiggling them as she came against Ohana's sucking mouth on her clit, against Ohana's slowly plunging fingers. Then she sagged in the furs, and Ohana kissed her thighs and moved away, returning to her spot near the fire.

• • • •

IN THE FALL THAT FOLLOWED, Varg gave birth to a healthy daughter she named Idunn. Dagdag and Idunn became fast friends, believing themselves to be sisters and not knowing they were also cousins. They were frequently seen running about the cave or screaming and chasing each other through the flower fields. And like their other half-sisters, they were both small versions of Ohana. They had the same white hair, and as they grew older, it became more and more apparent that they would be warriors rather than cave wives.

Firga was proud of her nieces and took part in training them, while Marmar told them stories of the lands beyond the Great Forest, and Suga warned the girls of the monstrous saber cats in the foothills and taught them what berries were safest to eat.

Ohana held the Snowy Mountains for another twenty years, and in that time, Varg gave her ten daughters – an eleventh died in childbirth and another died in the winter. With her twenty wives from various raids, the chieftess was now father to a healthy brood, but Ohana's favorite daughters by far were Dagdag and Idunn, who were now two young warriors quite eager to venture out and see the Great Forest for themselves.

One day, as Varg was sitting outside the cave and enjoying the summer sun, she held her youngest to her breasts, and as she was feeding the girl, Dagdag came marching up.

Dagdag was now a hard-bodied warrior, with long white hair and a dark stripe of war paint across her eyes, just like her father. She wore a hand-axe on each hip, and her skirt of furs and leathers swung around her bare legs as she marched up to Varg and stood over her.

"Where is my mother," Dagdag said without preamble.

Varg blinked, startled, and said in amusement, "Good morning to you as well, daughter."

Dagdag scowled. "You are *not* my mother, for Aunt Firga has told me the truth. So I ask again: where is my mother?! And why was she kept from me?"

Varg sighed, cursing Firga. The woman could never keep her mouth shut. She looked up again to find Dagdag still furious and waiting. Varg shrugged. "What is the use in knowing?" she said. "You should be focused on taking your first wife. How would it benefit you to know that your mother was exiled?"

Hearing that, Dagdag sagged miserably. "Exiled for what?" she asked unhappily.

"For betraying your father with another," Varg answered apologetically.

Dagdag blinked unhappily, then suddenly sat beside Varg, drawing up one knee and resting her elbow on it as she stared thoughtfully into the distance. Varg looked at Dagdag as she cradled her youngest to her breasts and thought the girl as beautiful and strong as her father.

"How could she do such a foolish thing?" Dagdag wondered and scowled, shaking her head.

"Love makes fools of us all," Varg whispered and felt a tear rise in her eye when she thought of little Frigg. Frigg would have been a woman by now. Was she even still alive?

Varg cleared her throat, pushing thoughts of Frigg aside. "Why don't you take a wife?" she asked Dagdag to change the subject. "The clan would respect your claim to chieftess more if you did."

Dagdag scoffed. "I do not want the women here. That's what I came to tell you, Mother."

Varg smiled to herself: so she was still Mother after all. But she looked around in horror when she realized what Dagdag had said. "You are too young to go raiding!" she protested.

Dagdag smiled wearily. "Oh, Mother! I'm a woman now! Besides, it isn't really a raid. When father took the Wolf clan, she left behind many children. Those children will be beautiful women by now, just wandering the forests, unmated. I shall steal them and claim six, seven wives in one go." She stood, her back to Varg as she said, "Wish me luck."

T he Sheep people were frightened. For there were fiery raids and bloody battles raging throughout the Great Forest, and there was fear that the battling clans would come to the foothills, as they always did.

Revna was not afraid. While her clan whispered and worried, she walked in the sunlight, pensive and yet day-dreamy. For every night, a fierce warrior came to her in her dreams and roughly took her, grabbing her long red hair from behind and ripping her fur dress open, then groping her bare breasts and fingering her throbbing sex there, in the high golden fields, until she blushed and trembled as she came, her shrill cries rising to the bright blue sky as she frowned in baffled delight.

The first night the dream warrior came, Revna was afraid, for the dream warrior was a big woman, tall and strong, with dark brown hair and fierce, slanted eyes. Like most warriors, she was grim and never smiled, though delight brightened her narrow eyes as they glanced over Revna's curvy body.

And then the dream warrior pounced like a wolf and ate her prey, slamming Revna on her back and snatching her thighs open before burying her face between. Revna had never lain with a woman before and had only given herself the pleasure, but in her dreams the pleasure was far more intense than anything her little fingers had ever done, her orgasms multiplying in waves as the dream warrior slowly sucked her clit as if savoring its taste and roughly fingered her with her strong, insistent fingers.

The dreams were so intense that Revna often cried out in her sleep and was embarrassed when she awoke wet and breathless beneath the moon, her big breasts heaving.

Revna was a beautiful young woman with wild red hair falling to her backside and freckles from the kiss of the sun. Like all the women of her clan, her face and arms were striped with blue clay from the river, marking her as one of the peaceful Sheep people.

The Sheep people did not believe in violence, and the consequence was that it made them vulnerable to raids from the more bloodthirsty and territorial clans. Revna herself was terrified of violence, fire, and destruction, but as a witch, her dreams often gifted her such visions.

It was Revna who often warned the clan that the violent clans were coming, but now, since her visions of the dream warrior had begun, she had decided not to warn them of the day it would happen. For she knew allowing the raiders to come was the only way she would ever be taken by the beautiful and hard-bodied warrior in her dreams.

Revna also just hated by her own clan. As a witch, she was often ostracized and treated as if she were dangerous or evil – especially when her moons came. It was believed that a witch's blood held a great and dangerous power, and so, whenever she bled, Revna was often forced to leave the clan and keep to herself in the hills at night.

Revna had no family, for she was a foundling and had not even been born of the clan. Typically, witches were stoned, and a stoning was almost Revna's fate when her powers manifested as a child. But the clan soon realized Revna's visions could be used to forestall danger, and so she was allowed to live –hated and ostracized, feared and ignored – but she was allowed to live, watching as feminine girls her own age became women and were taken by masculine sheepherder wives, while she always remained untouched and alone.

Well, now was Revna's chance to finally live the life she deserved. The dream warrior would come, and her powerful clan would ravage the camp, taking sheepherder femmes for wives while slaying their butch protectors. Then Revna would be taken by the young warrior and would become First Wife of a powerful chieftess. She had seen it all in her dreams and could barely contain her excitement.

It baffled Revna that the Sheep people had never thought she would use her visions to betray them. Perhaps they thought she would remain loyal, for her survival until that point that had depended on protecting her clan. But surely they would have realized that Revna also had leverage: she was a great beauty and she was feminine, young, and fertile. If the warriors came, they would never slay her but take her as a mate – so long as Revna kept her power a secret.

Oh, yes. Revna must run and scream and pretend to be horrified by the big warrior coming to making rough love to her. She mustn't let on that she knew the truth.

• • • •

LATER THAT NIGHT, AS the Sheep people camped under the stars in the open field, Revna was roughly shaken awake by one of the clanswomen. She dragged Revna upright by the shoulders and shook her, demanding to know why she hadn't warned them of the danger ahead of time.

Revna glanced past the clanswoman's wide, frightened eyes and held back a smirk: on the far side of the camp, fire was blazing, and feminine women were screaming as their masculine wives were cut down. Revna could already see the femmes hanging over the shoulders of their butch captors, legs kicking in defiance, as their lovers were felled.

The children and the elderly, of course, were spared, for it was not the way of warrior women to harm the helpless. Even the masculine sheepherders who peacefully surrendered their wives were allowed to live, though they would live with great shame.

Then Revna saw her: the dream warrior! She was a head taller than the rest, with long brown hair and fierce slanted eyes, just like in Revna's dream. She had not yet claimed a woman and seemed to be preoccupied with the thrill of battling the masculine sheepherders – or rather, cutting them down, for the masculine sheepherders were no warriors, had no weapons, and did not stand a chance. The dream warrior was like a wolf that had been let loose upon a den of rabbits.

She was slaying butch sheepherders left and right, and she was enjoying it.

Revna watched the dream warrior for a beat and felt her clit throb as the woman's rippling abs and cleavage glistened with sweat. Oh, yes. She was every bit as beautiful, powerful, and violent as the dream. Revna was in love.

"You let them come here, didn't you?" snarled the clanswoman, and she shook Revna roughly by the shoulders again. "I saw the way you looked at that *beast* who leads them! You're helping them, aren't you? Aren't you—?!"

Revna felt something in her snap, and she slapped the clanswoman across the face. She was smugly satisfied when the woman shrieked and dropped out of her sight.

Then it happened: the dream warrior heard the slap and looked right at Revna. She had buried her axe in a sheepherder's face and was in the middle of kicking the woman away when she saw Revna and did a doubletake. She went completely still, just staring at Revna, who couldn't move as she stared back, feeling like a mouse that a cat had spotted.

Revna was not afraid of the dream warrior, but she could not escape the feeling that the woman viewed her as prey or perhaps a prize, something to be gotten before some other warrior spotted it.

Eyes now fixed on Revna, the dream warrior ripped her axe free of the sheepherder (whose body collapsed as she turned away) and marched in a hard, confident stride toward Revna. She walked through fire, she walked through struggling warriors and screaming Sheep people, her eyes fixed unwaveringly on Revna.

Holding down another smirk, Revna jumped up, faked a frightened scream, and took off running toward the edge of the camp, where the fields spread away to the trees on the horizon. She almost giggled when the dream warrior broke into a run after her.

* * * *

FRIGG RAN, KEEPING her eyes fixed on the switching backside, the narrow waist, the bouncing breasts of the most beautiful woman she had ever seen. With her muscular, powerful legs, she knew she would overtake the redhead easily. Instead she paced her jog, allowing the redhead to reach the edge of the camp before finally dropping her axe and pouncing the woman from behind.

Frigg reached around and cupped the little woman's big breasts. They were large as melons, the cleavage nicely plump. Not full of milk. So she was not a mother. How was it so? She was young but not so young that she shouldn't have mated. Was she barren? Frigg was worried, but one look at the fat breasts in her hands and she didn't care.

Frigg tightened her hands and was prepared to rip the woman's dress open when the woman screamed and trembled, her little hands prying frantically at Frigg's bigger, stronger hands. She was begging in her language, she was crying. Yet even when she was crying, the redhead was unbelievably beautiful.

"Hush," Frigg whispered soothingly and kissed the redhead's cheek. She whispered in the woman's ear, "I will not harm you. I will not harm you."

The redhead must have understood, for she hiccoughed to silence, her big breasts trembling nicely in Frigg's hands. Frigg gently ripped the woman's dress open, allowing her bare breasts to push free. They were quite large and high and young, beautiful swollen breasts with tiny pink nipples. Frigg felt her clit throbbing just looking at them.

Unable to contain herself much longer, Frigg roughly turned the woman's face to her own, and as she kissed the little redhead over her shoulder, she cupped her heavy breasts from behind, a finger rotating each hard nipple.

The redhead trembled in the tatters of her fur dress, her big breasts bare above the fabric. She seemed unsure of what to do with her hands and awkwardly rested her arms atop Frigg's muscular arms – an adorable cluelessness. So she was a virgin. Good, Frigg thought, for there would be no angry wife coming to challenge her.

Still cupping and fingering one of the redhead's breasts, Frigg released the other and reached down and fingered her sex through the little swath of red hair there. It was tight and clenching and growing more moist by the minute, lengthening and allowing Frigg's fingers further access.

Frigg hooked two fingers inside and started roughly fingering – harder and faster, until the little redhead's hips were jerking. Her cheeks flamed as she was so forcefully fingered, and she frowned in baffled delight as she cried out and climaxed.

* * * *

FRIGG WAS MADLY IN lust with Revna to the point of wanting no other woman (which shocked her fellow warriors), but Hilgar wound not hear of it. After Frigg was abandoned by her mother as a child, in the melting snow of the Southern Great Forest, she and the other abandoned daughters were taken in by Hilgar, a wise and ancient woman who must've been the oldest woman in the entire forest.

Hilgar was a bony old woman with long, white hair in a messy plait down her back, a leather headband about her wrinkled forehead, and sagging muscles half-bulging in the leather and furs of a chieftess many seasons past her prime. She even still wore her handaxe and shield, for Hilgar used to be a warlord, raiding other clans, taking feminine women as wives. She had acted as a father, not a mother, to Frigg, a role model and a teacher and mentor when it came to weaponry and strategy. And because she was such a serious, grim, hard-ass, she never let up on Frigg, often giving her advice in her endeavors as a chieftess—whether Frigg wanted it or not.

Frigg loved Hilgar, but she was getting sick of her shit.

After growing into womanhood and spending many years training under Hilgar, Frigg had decided that she would form her own clan –

the Clan of the Wolf reborn – and that she would avenge her father, the powerful warlord and chieftess, Turaga, by taking all of the Great Forest for herself and destroying the mighty Cave Bear clan.

So far, Frigg had captured one of the Sheep clans, had taken the most beautiful woman for her wife, had pushed the Hawk clan out of the Southern Great Forest and taken its most ancient and fertile lands for herself. She had also chosen her best scouts and sent them out to spy upon the Bear clan, and in doing so, she had learned that the Bear clan was still following under the leadership of Ohana, but her daughter, Dagdag, was in the run for taking her place.

In fact, Dagdag had become such a mighty warrior that Frigg knew it was Ohana's favored daughter that she must target in her planned raid. As soon as she had the numbers, she would move on the Bear clan. She had already convinced some of the Hawk warriors to surrender and join her.

Anyone who overtook the Cave Bear clan would become the most powerful chieftess to walk the soil of the ancestors. Frigg was determined to be that chieftess, even taking on the war name Frigg the Fierce. Hilgar said it sounded ridiculous, but what did she know?

Everything was going well. The Hawk clan was defeated, the Deer clan would be taken next, and Revna was already growing big with child. Soon, Frigg would fulfill the prophecy and become a chieftess to be remembered throughout the ages.

Yes, everything was going well.

• • • •

REVNA BLUSHED AS HER own shrill screams of ecstasy filled the fur canvas of the tent. Frigg was on top of her in the dark room they shared, fingering Revna hard as she looked into her eyes, fingering her until the moisture was running down her trembling thighs. Revna thought her clit would burst for its throbbing. And then it happened: Frigg crammed her fingers in hard, hooking them upward, so that

Revna was forced to thrust her hips as she climaxed, Frigg's lips sucking hard upon her little pink nipple.

When Revna had sagged in the furs and was happily panting, Frigg showered her face, neck, and breasts with slow, wet, loving kisses. Revna closed her eyes and smiled and blindly touched Frigg's dark hair. The dream warrior was more than she ever could have asked for, a fierce protector and lover, which was why she felt so terribly guilty.

Revna had successfully hidden the fact that she was a witch from Frigg and the entire Wolf clan, but she had yet another secret that would cost her a stoning if Frigg learned of it.

As soon as Frigg was sleeping in the furs behind the curtain of their room, Revna crept from bed, pulling her fur dress on as she went, and entered the sitting room, where a fire was blazing low within a circle of stones. Here, she knelt beside the flames and outstretched her hand, turning the fire purple.

Almost instantly, Dagdag slipped inside the mouth of the tent and was upon her from behind – hot, feverish kisses, groping on her big breasts, ripping impatiently at the front of her fur dress, so that one of her breasts trembled free.

Dagdag managed to finger one of Revna's hard pink nipples before the witch got away, giggling as she crawled out of reach, and playing Hard to Get. She was on hands and knees, and one big tit was swinging down from her torn dress. She knew what she looked like to Dagdag, crawling away with her bulging sex bare between the back of her thighs. She giggled when she heard a moan of longing: she was tormenting poor Dagdag.

Dagdag pounced Revna from behind, hugging her about the waist and kissing her neck as her soft giggles continued. Then the hard-bodied warrior reached back, and gripping the back of Revna's neck, she forced the witch to leaned down, backside in the hair.

Revna's blushing cheek was now pressed to the sitting furs near the fire, and she moaned when Dagdag's fingers suddenly slid in her sex, gliding deep and strong and yet sensuously slow – Dagdag always did like to take her time. She was not a brute like Frigg, which excited Revna, for it was something new.

Clit throbbing with arousal, Revna moaned and clenched her sex on Dagdag's fingers as she was pleasured. She could already feel the moisture building again, and indeed, as her sex lengthened, Dagdag's fingers were able to slide deeper through its hot, heavy walls.

The deep, slow fingering went on for some time, and then Dagdag gave a choked cry and tried too late to pull her fingers free, while Revna realized with great dread and regret what was happening. She gasped as Dagdag's seed rushed from her fingers to fill her heaving sex, then she sat up, red hair streaming across her pretty eyes, and the lovers gazed at each other in horror.

• • • •

THE SPRING LASTED HALF the year, for the seasons in the Great Forest were long, and in the early days of Fall, Revna gave birth to a child with white hair and blue eyes. Frigg – who was dark in her aspect, with brown hair and dark eyes – was furious and shocked, for it could only mean one thing: Revna had lain with Dagdag, the child of the warlord Ohana.

Dagdag's line was quite ancient and powerful, and each woman born of it had white hair. There was a reason Ohana and now Dagdag were so mighty. There was a reason why Ohana's feminine daughters were so fair. They and they alone had the white hair – and now, so did Frigg's supposed child.

Hilgar was outraged on Frigg's behalf. She grabbed Revna by the hair and dragged her out into the center of the camp, in the center of the circle of stones, near the great fire, where the clan often gathered. There, within the circle of stones, Hilgar threw Revna down in the dirt and picked up a rock the size of an apple, preparing to kill her.

Others began to gather, curious and whispering, gasping and shocked. Hilgar pointed a finger at Revna (who knelt in the dirt with her red hair streaming wild to hide her face) and then shouted to the gathering crowds, "This woman is a traitor, for she has lain with our enemy!"

More gasping and whispering. Then angry warriors stepped forward, and they too picked up stones. The stoning was about to begin when Frigg suddenly arrived and called it to a halt. She marched into the circle of stones, carrying Revna's whitehaired daughter in a bundle in her arms.

Revna was so relieved that she silently wept behind her hair as Frigg stood protectively in front of her. Frigg announced to the gathered clan that she loved Revna too greatly to slay her for her trespass, but she would gladly slay the babe, who she then lifted in the air by the heel.

The tiny infant began to scream as its fur blanket fell away, and Revna, horrified as Frigg lifted her axe, threw herself at the woman's feet and begged for mercy. She hated how coldly Frigg looked down at her, how the woman's eyes sneered with disgust. For an instant, it seemed as if Frigg would indeed slay Revna's child, and then – to Revna's great surprise – Hilgar spoke up.

"This is beneath you, Frigg," Hilgar quietly said. "Children are innocent. Only cowards do slay them. Do not punish the child for the sin of the mother."

Frigg glared over her shoulder at Hilgar, then looked uncertainly at the screaming child, who she still held aloft by the heel. Revna was relieved to see the guilt fill Frigg's dark eyes and her arm slightly lower the child. She was wavering.

"Raise your enemy's child to destroy your enemy," Hilgar said in her stern, cold voice. She was standing, arms folded, behind Frigg as she spoke. "Or sell her to be the village whore in some other clan," she added nonchalantly, and Revna angrily gasped. "She is more useful to you alive, for she is likely to be a witch after her mother, and we of the Wolf use witches. We do not slay them."

Revna blinked in surprise. She had not know the Wolf clan held no malice for witches. She'd thought all the clans hated them. She looked around at the gather clanswomen with new eyes and wondered if she could have, in fact, garnered her respect had she not strayed.

Revna had believed herself to be suspected and hated for what she was, and so, her belief became true as she isolated herself and became withdrawn, fearing that her secret would be exposed. This led to the clanswomen not trustng her. It also led to her long walks alone in the forest, where she met the beautiful and fierce Dagdag, who came up behind and – after Revna smiled flirtatiously—without a word, made love to her.

Revna felt eyes upon her and looked around to find Hilgar glaring at her with a startling amount of hatred. Had the old warrior always known Revna was a witch? And if so, why hadn't Hilgar exposed her? If witches were valuable tools to the Wolf clan, it would have made more sense for Hilgar to have told Frigg the truth of Revna's nature. Instead, she had kept Revna's secret for months on end.

Having made her decision, Frigg turned to Revna, leaned down, and placed the wailing babe in her arms. The child stopped screaming immediately, and Revna kissed its head in great relief. Then she looked up and said miserably, "My Frigg, I will never betray you a—Ah!"

Frigg's hand came down so hard, Revna's head snapped to the side. She gave a choked scream of shock as she was stricken, and she felt a tooth rip painfully from her mouth. As the blood spattered hot down her lip, she saw her tooth roll across the dirt like a white stone before stopping, red flesh and blood hanging ragged from it.

Trembling all over with rage, mouth pulsing with pain, Revna bowed her head behind her hair in bitter submission as Frigg hissed, "If you *ever* spread your legs for another woman *again*, I will kill you."

• • • •

FRIGG FOUND IT BAFFLING that she had gone from loving Revna fiercely to hating her with a passion. She was beginning to suspect that the witch had cast a spell on her. She had known all along that Revna was a witch, for she had dreamt of her before even meeting her, and the ancestors seemed to want her to take Revna as her mate. But why?

Why did the ancestors smile on Revna when the witch was a traitor? She did not love Frigg. Perhaps she had never loved Frigg and had only used her. The woman had unapologetically slept with the daughter of Frigg's great enemy and bore the hated Dagdag's child, while hoping to pass it off as belonging to Frigg!

Frigg wanted to hit Revna some more, wanted to beat her into bloody submission and make her so ugly that no other woman would ever want her again – but Hilgar told her to stay her hand.

Hilgar told Frigg that if she hated the mother so, then she should just kill her and give the child to another woman to suckle. According to Hilgar, there was no reason beyond cruelty to keep a traitorous woman around just to beat on her.

If she were sent away and allowed to live, Revna could not survive the coming winter on her own. And if she went to live with the Bear clan, then she would be lending her magick power and strength to Ohana and ensuring her continued rule of the Great Forest. No, cautioned Hilgar, it were better to slay Revna and be done with her.

That night, Frigg decided she would lead Revna into the forest and kill her there, away from the clan. Then in the morning, the clan would pack up and move on, following the mammoth herds.

Axe in hand, Frigg led Revna by the upper arm into the trees. Revna was weeping and clutching the tiny whitehaired babe in her arms. She had already guessed what would happen but had insisted on bringing the babe to die with her as well. Frigg didn't care. She would cut the thing in halves like kindling. It wasn't hers.

When they had traveled deeply enough into the forest so that they would not be seen – but could still see the camp – Frigg stopped and turned to face Revna. The child began to wail. Frigg was about to lift her axe and cleave Revna's face in two when a heavy blade suddenly sank in the back of her skull with a dull crunch, there was a spatter of dark blood across the fallen leaves, and Frigg's mouth fell open as red lines poured from her eyes.

• • • •

REVNA WASN'T SURPRISED to see Dagdag standing there, for she'd had a dream that her lover would come and save her. She had only pretended to weep the better to fool Frigg. So, apparently, had the babe, for it stopped weeping as soon as its father was near and gazed up at big, powerful Dagdag in quiet wonder.

Dagdag was as beautiful as ever, a tall woman with powerful shoulders and bulging arms, standing two heads taller than little Revna, a handaxe in her fist. Her long white hair had been pulled back in the center in a long plait while the rest hung loose and wild about her shoulders, and she had a stripe of dark muddy warpaint across her slanted eyes. She looked just like her father, Ohana.

Dagdag's eyes were fixed in concern on Revna's face. "Are you all right, Moon of my Heart?"

Revna smiled at the endearment. Dagdag was sweet and strong and gentle and would never hurt her, even if she strayed. She was a much better mate than Frigg had ever been. Indeed, Frigg had been evil and cruel, willing to murder her child to punish her!

Perhaps Frigg had simply been a stepping stone to true happiness. Revna was looking forward to her new life with the Bear clan.

"She's so tiny," said Dagdag, who was looking down at the babe in Revna's arms in quiet awe. She leaned down and kissed the child on the head, and the child giggled in response.

Dagdag gazed fondly at the babe for a beat, then she straightened up and offered her hand, gazing down at Revna with such affection, Revna's heart warmed.

"Come, wife," said Dagdag, offering her hand. "You belong with me now."

Revna smiled and took Dagdag's hand in her own. Then the two of them walked off into the forest, leaving Frigg's prone body in a pool of blood.

A strid, Dagdag and Revna's eldest daughter, was a woman now. And not only that, but a mighty sorceress whose power could lend its might to the Bear clan, just as Ohana had always hoped, much to Dagdag's irritation. For Astrid was Dagdag's favorite child and thus, Dagdag was loath marry her off.

But they needed the alliance. The Deer people, despite their gentle name, were a formidable people who held the corner of the Great Forest with the most abundant deer. They had held those sacred lands since the beginning of time, having been chosen by the gods themselves to guard them. So it was that every chieftess in the Great Forest respected the Deer clan and would not invade them by force.

No. The only way to secure access to those hunting grounds without stirring the wrath of the gods was marriage, and Astrid was the most beautiful flower in the Great Forest.

Ohana was determined to see it happen before she passed on to the Endless Fields. It was the final piece of her forest chiefdom, her legacy.

For Ohana, in her winter years, had stepped down from her chiefdom, leaving her throne of rock to Dagdag, and was now Dagdag's advisor in all things war.

Of course, Ohana's other warrior children did not take this lightly. Dagdag was challenged on all sides by her masculine sisters, who thought they would make better rulers over the Great Forest, and Dagdag was shocked to sorrow when even Idunn stepped up to challenge her. But all fought Dagdag and all of them fell.

Varg, now an old woman with silver hair, told Dagdag that her mother would be proud. Dagdag replied that Varg was her mother, not this Tara whom she had never known, never would know. To her surprise, Varg seemed hurt by the dismissal of her exiled sister, but the old woman did not argue, instead returning to her coveted place on Ohana's knee.

Ohana was proud of Dagdag and had never dreamed that her child with the Exile could prove so formidable. She was sorry to see the death of Idunn, and a grand funeral pyre was built for the girl, but Ohana would be a liar if she pretended Dagdag were not her favorite child.

Unfortunately, though a great warrior, Dagdag did not possess the hunger and drive for power and land that a chieftess was supposed to. Instead, she spent far too long mourning those she defeated, and she fought angrily against any suggestion from Revna that Astrid should marry.

Thankfully, Revna and Astrid combined had a drive for power and might that more than made up for Dagdag's lack of it. Ohana never thought she would side with foul witches, but they were clever women who wanted power and riches as much as Ohana. And not just that – there was security to consider.

Though Dagdag had defeated and conquered the other clans, she had been too merciful, and many Wolf clan warriors were still alive, still plotting revenge – especially with the death of Frigg, who they had considered some sort of omen at her birth.

Finally, it was Varg who swayed Dagdag's stubborn heart with the magic words, "Idunn would want this."

Dagdag then had to concede that Idunn would, in fact, want to see the Bear clan thrive. The young chieftess succumbed to her gentle aunt-mother, and Astrid was promised to the people of the Deer.

• • • •

YOUNG MORDAR HAD YELLOW hair and blue eyes and was muscular and big as a mammoth. She had been chieftess since her great father's passing, but she was yet to take a wife. There simply weren't any beautiful enough, she grunted while looking with great indifference upon the many lovely young things that paraded before her.

There wasn't a lack of young, nubile women in the Great Forest. Clans everywhere wanted access to the tawny yellow deer, a succulent delicacy, and so, they sent their women from far and wide.

Some of the clans that had been conquered by Ohana even went behind Dagdag's back and sent women to Mordar, hoping to form an alliance. Mordar didn't blame them, for any alliance with her clan would ensure a winter's supply of food, which would mean independence from Dagdag's Bear clan.

But none of the women sent to her were beautiful enough, Mordar complained, and that night she went to bed in a foul mood.

Mordar awoke again when there was movement in the dark curtained room of her tent. Her strong hand went immediately to one of the daggers on her hip and had curled into a hard fist around the hilt when the curtain rustled, and by the firelight beyond, Mordar caught the hourglass silhouette of a woman.

"Who is there?" Mordar called hoarsely.

"Only your wife," answered an amused voice.

Mordar went still as the curtain fell back into place, shutting out the firelight and plunging her in darkness once more. There was a pause, a whisper, then an orb of golden light appeared in the woman's hands, reddening the tips of her slender fingers and setting her face aglow. She let the wisp of light drift to the ceiling, and as it did, its light shed over the woman, illuminating her before Mordar like some visiting goddess.

Mordar felt her throat run dry, felt her heart quicken, felt a pulse in her sex, for the stranger was the most beautiful woman Mordar had ever seen.

The woman stood in a fur gown that clung to her curves, accentuating her round hips, narrow waist, and ample breasts. The garment was not crude but finely tailored, suggesting the wealth of her clan. But it was obvious by the color of her white hair who she was: Astrid, the daughter of Dagdag.

Ohana had been after Mordar for months to mate with her granddaughter, and had Mordar known what Astrid looked like, she might have accepted long before. She had assumed the legend of Astrid's beauty a myth until that moment.

Smirking into Mordar's smitten eyes, Astrid let her gown drop away, revealing her curvy body, her slender belly, long legs, and large, plump breasts that were jutting with tiny pink nipples. With swaying hips, she lowered herself down on all fours, and with her great breasts swinging, she crawled across the sheepskins to Mordar, who was still leaning in shock on her elbow.

Astrid laid her soft, warm body atop Mordar's hard muscular one, pressing her great breasts against Mordar's. Then she smiled again, and curling her fingers firmly in Mordar's long yellow hair, she kissed her hungrily on her mouth.

Mordar grunted in surprise but melted into the kiss, and she did not argue when Astrid, with jiggling breasts, sat up and pushed Mordar down on the furs. Then she closed her hot thighs around Mordar's face, and Mordar felt her sex throbbing when the hot, moist lips pressed against her mouth.

Mordar had pleased many women, and so, her eager mouth effortlessly brought Astrid to wiggling and gasping, twisting her round hips and sliding her wet sex against Mordar's sucking lips and gliding tongue.

At last, Astrid dropped her head back and trembled as she climaxed, and Mordar watched the undersides of her big breasts thrust. Grunting as she also climaxed, Mordar reached up and groped hard at Astrid's big, heaving breasts. The nipples jutted hard in her fists, and she wanted to suck them.

Without warning, Mordar grabbed Astrid by her narrow waist and rolled on top of her. Astrid giggled like a girl, but her giggles subsided to helpless moans when Mordar buried her face between her thighs, burrowing her mouth and flexing her chin, her fists groping all the while at Astrid's breasts

Astrid thrust her breasts and gasped, her pretty eyes fluttering wide as Mordar strokes her strong fingers deep inside her heaving walls. Astrid's sex clenched as Mordar's seed filled her, and then she lay there in the nest of her long white hair, happy and panting, big breasts heaving. She giggled again – such a pretty sound, Mordar thought with delight – as Mordar trailed devoted kisses up her body, and when their lips touched, her kiss was as hungry as before.

"I am yours," Astrid whispered, closing her slender arms around Mordar's thick neck.

"You are mine," Mordar agreed and sucked long and slow on Astrid's nipple, making her moan.

● ● ● ●

ASTRID AND MORDAR WERE married by the clan priestess the next morning, and it wasn't long before Astrid was with child, her belly growing steadily rounder.

Mordar was so in love that she declared she would never take another wife. Her advisor, Ulga, called her a fool and reminded her that she would need to make many fine heirs and warriors – and witches did not make warriors. No, they made cave wives.

But Mordar ignored Ulga's warnings and did as she pleased. And yet, it was to her great frustration that her wife never produced warrior-daughters, instead giving birth to three feminine witches who looked just like Dagdag, with white hair and piercing eyes.

The Bear clan bloodline had prevailed. None of Mordar's children even looked like her, let alone could wield a blade. Mordar was furious, for it was a great embarrassment to have her seed appear weak. The other warrior women were laughing behind her back. It was time to act or lose her place as chieftess.

And so, when Astrid was pregnant with her fourth child, in the dead of winter, Mordar threw her out of their stone house and into the snow. Astrid begged and cried, so sweet and pretty, on her knees and surrounded by her sobbing daughters, but Mordar would hear none of it. She accused Astrid of manipulating her with witchcraft, of using her to create more witches. Witches could not be trusted, Mordar bellowed, yellow hair streaming across her angry eyes.

And so, with the village watching from their houses, Astrid trekked into the snow, large with child, her three daughters weeping as they followed.

· · · ·

DAGDAG WAS FURIOUS when she learned of what had happened to her daughter. So was Revna, who wanted revenge. Poor Astrid had disappeared into the Great Forest and had not been seen or heard of in days. Dagdag feared her death and secretly wept where no one could see, in the dark of her stone home, while Revna kissed her head.

Because they had formed an alliance with the Deer people, the Bear clan had been able to come down from the mountain and build homes, no longer forced to follow the mammoth herds, as they now had access to the yellow deer. As a result, Dagdag had built her wives a fine and sturdy home, as had the other warrior women in the clan, and there was much talk of expansion across the sea.

But now, all of that would end if the alliance with the Deer people fell through. Dagdag was at a loss. If they took vengeance and spilled blood on sacred land, the gods would be displeased. Revna suggested that they lure Mordar out of her protected lands to a place where she would be vulnerable.

"Of course," Dagdag realized. "Mordar is a dog. She can be lured out, pussy throbbing, by a young pair of tits."

"But whose pair of tits?" Revna said thoughtfully. She met Dagdag's eye and knew she was thinking along the same lines.

As their plan came together, the lovers smiled and kissed.

• • • •

ARUH SAT IN THE SNOW, shivering, just beyond the edge of the Deer clan's sacred lands, just as she'd been told. She had been promised to become one of Dagdag's wives, taken care of the rest of her life if she would but spread her thighs and allow Chieftess Mordar to go down on her. She must pretend to be in awe and play on Mordar's ego. For Mordar was a picky woman who lost interest easily.

Aruh thought it all a bizarre request, but there was no higher station a femme wife could have beyond marrying a chieftess, and Dagdag was the mightiest chieftess in the Great Forest. Aruh would be taken care of and know rich meats and fine furs the rest of her life. Her mother asked her how she could say no, and though Aruh's mother hated her, Aruh agreed with the old woman. Whatever the reason, she must seduce Mordar and secure a life of riches with Dagdag.

Aruh sat in the snow, long red hair flowing about hershivering, one of her breasts poking bare from the tear in her fur dress. Dagdag had torn her dress and rubbed mud on her body, the better to make Aruh seem pitiful and distressed. Then Dagdag told Aruh to scream and retreated into the trees.

Aruh obeyed, screaming and pretending to sob, screaming that she was lost and frightened.

A few minutes later, and boots crunched the snow. Aruh went still. Chieftess Mordar was coming, but she wasn't alone! This hadn't been part of the plan!

Aruh watched as the two big warrior women approached through the trees. They were tall, as all warrior women were tall, and they carried axes on their shoulders. They appeared to be talking in low voices, arguing about something.

Chieftess Mordar lumbered along, long blonde hair framing a scowl. She appeared irritated. Besides her, her silver-haired companion was scolding her.

"—should let her die in the wilderness," the older woman was saying crossly, her long silver plait flowing behind her. "It was foolish to leave the holy ground—"

"How many times have I told you not to call me a fool, Ulga?" Mordar snapped. "I heard a scream, and if Astrid is hurt, I shall defend her—"

"Hurt?" snorted the apparent Ulga. "She is a mighty sorceress. Nothing can harm her except that she would allow it. This is some trap, I tell you—"

It was then that they noticed Aruh and stopped short.

Nervous, Aruh took a shaky breath and blushed as she said, "I have fled my clan to join yours after hearing of your might." She folded forward, touching her forehead to the snow. "Please claim me as your wife, mighty and strong Chieftess Mordar!"

There was a long pause as Aruh waited, folded forward on her knees. Then at last, Mordar spoke, "You are not pretty enough to be my wife....but you are pretty enough to fuck."

Aruh kept her face hidden as she blushed angrily.

"You need a new wife," Ulga scolded. She gestured at Aruh where she crouched in the snow. "Take this young thing."

"But how young is she?" Mordar said suggestively. She nodded at Aruh, who heard boots crunch toward her in the snow. A fist curled in her hair, and she was gently guided upright, so that she was kneeling. Ulga had sat her up, and now the big woman moved behind Aruh and roughly ripped her dress open, straight down the middle.

Aruh gasped and blushed as her perky little breasts shivered free. She cupped them to hide them, which did nothing to make them less appealing. She was confused when Ulga whispered in her ear, "Spread your thighs."

Trembling all over, Aruh obeyed, sitting back off her knees and spreading her legs to expose her sex. Her dress hung in tatters around her naked body, and though she kept her eyes down, she could feel Mordar staring at her like a beam of sunlight.

Mordar jerked her head, and with a serious glint in her eye, Ulga pinned Aruh on her back by the wrists. She leaned over Aruh, peering steadily down into her face, silently warning her not to move.

Aruh obeyed the silent command, breathing more rapidly from nerves, so that her perky breasts rode. She closed her eyes, wondering what to expect. She could feel Mordar's head between her thighs, the soft brisk of her hair, and then – Aruh gasped as Mordar's hungry lips and tongue sucked and glided over her sex.

Aruh cried out as her sex throbbed to life. Her pretty eyes fluttered wide in baffled pleasure, and when she glanced up,cot was to see Ulga watching her, eyes narrowed in lust.

Ulga leaned down and sucked deeply on one of Aruh's sharp tits, her hard hands still holding Aruh's wrists to the snow even as Mordar's hard hand held Aruh's shivering thighs in place.

Now both women were pleasuring Aruh, one's head between her thighs and the other buried in her tit, and trapped between them, Aruh shivered and moaned, her helpless cries ringing through the trees – until the pleasure suddenly stopped.

Aruh felt something hot splatter her skin. Confused, she looked down and screamed: Dagdag was standing over Mordar and had buried an axe in the back of her skull.

Cursing the Bear clan, Ulga reached for her axe, but Dagdag was faster. The White Bear ripped her axe with a nasty squelch from Mordar's hair and swung it again, bringing it down in Ulga's twisted face.

Dagdag ripped the axe free, and Ulga collapsed in a spray of snow, now dead.

Aruh sat up, shaken by what had happened and clutching her torn fur dress to her body. She was about to speak when she felt an incredible pain twisting her bones. She tried to scream and only a squeak came out. The trees were shooting higher and higher, growing larger, the moon disappearing beyond them.

Horrified, Aruh looked down and squeaked again. She had paws – white paws!

"Need you have turned the girl into a rabbit?" scolded Dagdag.

"As if I would have let you marry her," said Revna, stepping into view. She smirked. "Let's skin and eat her."

Aruh didn't wait to be skinned and eaten. She turned and took off as fast as her springy legs would allow.

When Aruh awoke, she was human again, and she was in a dimly lit cave, she was naked, and her wrists and ankles were bound to the wall, spread wide apart like a star. She blushed when she felt the cool air against her sex, which was exposed between her shapely thighs.

Glancing around through streams of red hair, Aruh could see that someone had made the cave their home. Her heart began to beat hard in fear, for only witches made their homes in meager caves these days. The clans had settled down and were growing from hide tents to stone fortresses. The first ever castle had been built to Dagdag at the heart of the first city, Villanhof.

The cave certainly showed signs of a witch's presence. There were skulls and bones everywhere, hanging herbs and entrails, and on the fire was a cauldron.

Standing over the cauldron, her face lit from under, was one of the most beautiful women Aruh had ever seen. Her hourglass body was scantily covered in hides and bones, and her great breasts were cradled by the bones of some fallen for. She smiled at Aruh from twin curtains of long dark hair, and her eyes reflected the firelight like candles.

"You are fortunate that I found you," the witch said, stirring her bone-handled spoon in the cauldron. She pulled the lade free of the dripping liquid and seductively licked it clean, dragging her pink tongue expertly along the curve. Aruh felt her clitoris swell just watching.

"My name is Hilgara," the witch said, striding over with high breasts and swaying hips, "and I will give you sanctuary here, little bunny, on one condition."

Aruh waited nervously. Witches were always asking for fingers, blood, or firstborn children.

"You must become my pet," Hilgara said at last.

Aruh felt relief flood through her. That didn't sound so bad. In fact, she might just enjoy it.

"I-If I say no?" Aruh weakly managed.

"Then you are free to try your luck out there in the wilderness," Hilgara answered. She moved closer, until she was face to face with Aruh, who hung still on the wall like a star. "Do we have an accord?" the witch asked, lifting an eyebrow.

"Y-Yes," Aruh managed hoarsely. She hadn't spoken in so long now that it felt odd to speak, almost painful, and there was still the faint squeak of a rabbit in her voice. Perhaps Revna's spell was still wearing off.

Hilgara smiled, very pleased. "Good girl," she said with great approval. "Smart girl."

The witch stepped very close now, so close that her hot breath tickled Aruh's lips. And then, without warning, she was kissing Aruh hard and hungry on the mouth, her head twisting.

Aruh's sex pulsed with her heartbeat: the witch was an incredible kisser. And now she felt the bone-handled of the spoon gliding slowly in her sex – lightly at first, and then deeper, faster, so that Aruh's sex grew moist and clenched strong on the handle. This pleased the witch, who pulled away to smile.

Aruh felt an ache in her chest when Hilgara's sweet mouth left her own. She moaned in complaint but quickly fell silent again when she realized what was happening: Hilgara knelt down, and Aruh trembled out a breathless cry when the witch sucked on her clitoris and the lips of her sex – slowly, deeply, deliciously – all the while stroking Aruh deep inside with the bone-handle.

Helplessly tied to the wall, Aruh blushed and cried out as her passion over spilled against the witch's sucking mouth.

• • • •

ARUH LIKED BEING THE witch's plaything. Hilgara taught Aruh how to hunt, how to make love, and even how to perform magick, so that by the time Spring rolled around, Aruh was self-sufficient and may have stricken out on her own, except she loved Hilgara, her mistress, far too greatly to ever leave her.

It was when she was out hunting that Aruh came face to face with Rocknar, one of the many warrior daughters of Dagdag.

It was said that a sorceress could produce only feminine daughters – a silly superstition, for Dagdag and Revna had many masculine warrior daughters. Chief Mordar's advisor had likely just wanted Astrid gone because she feared the sorceress and her growing importance at court, nothing more.

Aruh was now a sorceress herself, though never so powerful as Hilgara or Revna. She only knew a few meager spells and knew that if Rocknar decided to throw one of her axes, she would be dead before she could blink. So Aruh stood there frozen and frightened, her bow lowered, while Rocknar stared her down.

Rocknar looked as the rest of her father's bloodline: beautiful, big and tall, with long white hair and bulging arms. She carried an axe in each hand, down at her sides, her fur loincloth rippling in the cool breeze.

For the longest time, Rocknar merely pierced Aruh with her steady gaze. Then the warrior princess spoke, "You are Aruh. My father was to marry you but Mother turned you into a rodent. Don't trouble yourself so. I have not come to slay you. I am not so cruel as that."

Aruh let out a relieved breath. "Then why come you so deep in the forest, princess?"

"Father has tasked me with finding my sister. I have tracked her thus far but lost her trail at the river. Have you not seen her?"

"No," Aruh answered.

"Then what use are you? Perhaps I shall tell my mother I have seen you—"

"Wait, sweet princess! Keep our meeting secret and I will tell you of the most beautiful woman in the Great Forest and how you might make her wife."

Rocknar went still and listened.

· · · ·

THAT NIGHT, ARUH TOLD Hilgara of her meeting with Rocknar. The two of them lay together on a pallet of fires beside the fire, and tall, shapely Hilgara held little Aruh to her breasts.

Aruh cuddled close to her love, enjoying the sight of Hilgara's naked hip rising in the warm glow of fire and the dance of shadows. She could see that Hilgara was mulling over what Aruh had told her. The witch was likely seeing into the future, for her eyes were distant.

At last, Hilgara spoke. "Rocknar will bridenap a wife. Hmm. A most lovely flower. Dagdag will rule the Great Forest for fifty years. Hmm. Long-lived for a chieftess," she said, confirming Aruh's suspicions. "And the little sorceress Astrid, she shall rule the Deer people at Dagdag's bidding. The entire White Bear bloodline shall rule the forest . . . For better or worse."

"I don't care about them," Aruh complained. "What shall happen to us?"

Hilgara smiled. "You shall stay where the gods have placed you: at my side," she said, kissing Aruh's neck. "I knew I would love you the moment I saw you," she said between kisses.

Hilgara's kisses traveled down and down. She paused to suck tenderly on Aruh's pink nipples, which grew rigid in her lips. Aruh moan as the woman's kisses traveled lower.

Hilgara kisses Aruh's thighs and bowed her head between. Aruh moaned and thrust her breasts to her cave ceiling. They lifted, perky and plump, the nipples hard, and as she was going down on Aruh, Hilgara reached up and caressed her breasts, thumbing the nipples, then massaging the soft flesh.

Aruh wiggled and moaned as her breasts were caressed and her sex sucked. Her clitoris was throbbing so hard, she knew she would climax soon. With a helpless grown, she thrust her breasts against Hilgara's massaging hands and cried out weakly as she came.

Don't miss out!

Visit the website below and you can sign up to receive emails whenever Ash Gray publishes a new book. There's no charge and no obligation.

https://books2read.com/r/B-A-ZRKF-XFZXC

BOOKS2READ

Connecting independent readers to independent writers.

Did you love *Clan of the Cave Bear: The Complete Series*? Then you should read *Knights of Passion: The Complete Series*[1] by Ash Gray!

Zelda is a young feminine sorceress set to graduate from the tower and head out into the world for the first time on her own. Assigned as her guardian is butch knight Calain, a powerful warrior who is passionate, hot-headed, and a bit over-protective. When the queen of Eriallon attempts to force her affections on Zelda, Calain defends her lady without hesitation. The lovers are exiled, and with the aid of Calain's fellow knights, they escape into the realm on a grand adventure of passion, pleasure, and danger!

Knights of Passion: The Complete Series contains all ten of the original novellas, as well the short stories *The Fairy Ring, The Main*

---

1. https://books2read.com/u/b6aB9y

2. https://books2read.com/u/b6aB9y

Course, and *Aereth's Return.* Have a hard copy on your nightstand and enjoy a steamy read under the covers!

Also by Ash Gray

A Time of Darkness
Time's Arrow
The Infinite Athenaeum

Clan of the Cave Bear
Taken by the Chieftess
Passed Around
Keeping Warm
Her Pretty Pet
Dominated
Seduced
Caught
Clan of the Cave Bear: The Complete Series

Cyber Mech
Good With Her Hands

Fallen Stars

Fragile Hearts
Broken Minds
Digital Heartbeats
Electric Souls
Metal Bones

Her First Knight
The Knight of the Wild
Sparrow Song
Rowan's Hammer
The Dragon of Almara
Sanctuary
The Flower of Adwean
The Halls of Erinyel
The Daughter of Light
The Tomb of Azmon
Queen Liadan

Knight of Fire
The Queen of Swords
The Three of Goblets
The Queen of Wands
The Queen of Goblets
The Star
The World

Knights of Passion
The Queen's Lust

Handfasting the Warrior Queen
The Revenge of Raven's Cross
The Light of Lythara
Taming the Wolf Knight
The Mermaids of Menosea
The Fairy Queen of Elwenhal
The Dragon of Edhen
Essential Selene
Hearth and Home
Aereth's Return
The Fairy Ring
The Main Course
Knights of Passion: The Complete Series

Knights of Vallor
Saving Salia
Raven Spirit
Eryet's Fountain
The Daughter of Idet
The Mirror of Iovar
Aine's Athenaeum
Bone and Fire
Princess Eydis

Ona of Ozmora
The Amulet of Tizra
The Bandit Queen of Crystal Falls
The Council of Eldor
The Sword of Avara
Wicked Things in the Wilds

Pirates of Artusa
Stolen Booty
Taking Her Sword
Marooned
Wil's Way

Tales of the Blood Moon Coven
Bloodlust
The Hidden Memory
Whispered Names
Morbid Fascination
Bending to Her Will
Blood Rage
Prey
Hunted
Voyeuristic Intentions
Interludes and Ecstasy

The Assassin's Kiss
Crossed Daggers
Swordplay
Running Hot

The Chronicles of Omicron
The Thieves of Nottica
The Watchtower of Rustoria

The Dragon Riders of Valheera
Birthday Surprises

The Dreamscape
Out of Mind
Recalling Color

The Last Queen of Qorlec
Project Mothership
The Harvest
The Suns of Anarchy
The Light-year Lion
Moon Fire
Exiled Stars
Zora's Stone

The Legend of Kiva
The Starlight Stair

The Pussycat Chronicles
The Heist
Broken Hearts and Brain Damage
Candy, Sweat, and Regret
Lip Gloss and Loose Women

The Vampire's Seduction
First Taste
Bound
Turned

Witch Xim
Rezzora's Workshop

Standalone
Qorth
Fall Apart World
Unicorn Blood

About the Author

Ash Gray is a lesbian living in California. She writes lesfic (aka fiction for lesbians) in science fiction, fantasy, and paranormal settings.